KB085295

발칸의 장미를 내게 주었네

아시아에서는 《바이링궐 에디션 한국 대표 소설》을 기획하여 한국의 우수한 문학을 주제별로 엄선해 국내외 독자들에게 소개합니다. 이 기획은 국내외 우수한 번역가들이 참여하여 원작의 품격을 최대한 살렸습니다. 문학을 통해 아시아의 정체성과 가치를 살피는 데 주력해 온 아시아는 한국인의 삶을 넓고 깊게 이해하는 데 이 기획이 기여하기를 기대합니다.

Asia Publishers presents some of the very best modern Korean literature to readers worldwide through its new Korean literature series 〈Bilingual Edition Modern Korean Literature〉. We are proud and happy to offer it in the most authoritative translation by renowned translators of Korean literature. We hope that this series helps to build solid bridges between citizens of the world and Koreans through a rich in-depth understanding of Korea.

바이링궐 에디션 한국 대표 소설 072

Bi-lingual Edition Modern Korean Literature 072

He Gave Me Roses of the Balkans

정미경
발칸의 장미를 내게 주었네

Jung Mi-kyung

ASIA
PUBLISHERS

Contents

발칸의 장미를 내게 주었네

He Gave Me Roses of the Balkans

"가장 좋았던 건 뭐였어요?"

재이가 커피메이커에서 포트를 꺼내며 묻는다. 그 순간 열판 위에 커피 한 방울이 떨어진다. 치이익. 재이는 뜨거운 커피가 떨어진 게 제 이마이기라도 하듯 미간을 살짝 찌푸린다.

"비가 왔었어. 항구도시들은 다른 얼굴로 있다가도 비만 오면 모두 비슷한 풍경으로 바뀌는 거 같아. 함부르크, 샌프란시스코, 여수, 시모노세키. 맑은 날 보면 그토록 다른 도시들이 비가 오면 같은 표정을 짓거든. 비냄새, 바다냄새, 바다 위로 빗방울이 스미는 풍경, 그런 것들 때문일까? 피셔먼스 워프에 나갔었어. 해안가의 씨

"What did you like the most?"

Jae-i asked him as she took the pot from out of the coffee maker. Right then, a drop of coffee fell on the hot plate with a hiss. Jae-i frowned slightly, as if it had fallen on her forehead instead.

"It rained. All port cities are different, but I think they all become similar when it rains. Hamburg, San Francisco, Yeosu, Shimonoseki. On clear days, they all have such different faces, but then on rainy days, it's like they all put on the same expressions. The scent of rain, the sea, and the way raindrops seep into the sea... Maybe those are what make them all look the same. I went to Fisherman's

푸드 레스토랑에서 먹었던 클램차우더 수프야. 비오는 날, 퍼셔먼스 워프에서 먹었던 클램차우더 수프. 그게 제일 좋았어."

아득한 눈빛으로 그렇게 말하는 남자를 보며, 재이는 약간 뜻밖이라는 표정을 짓는다. 지난 여행에서 무엇이 가장 좋았던가 하는 건 개인적인 취향의 문제이긴 하지만 대체로 무심코 했던 비슷한 질문에 수프 따위를 말한 사람은 없었다.

하긴 사람들이 지난 여행에서 기억하는 게, 완벽한 아름다움을 자랑하는 고딕성당의 실루엣이나 비명 같은 탄성을 자아내던 풍경만은 아닌가 보다. 이름 모를 거리를 걸어가다 부딪친 낡은 돌담 사이에 피어 있던 노란 들꽃 한 송이, 혹은 버스가 모퉁이를 돌 때 스쳐 지났던 찻집의 올리브빛 테이블클로스의 기억, 그런 것들을 얘기했던 사람도 있었던 것 같다.

"클램차우더 수프가 뭐지?"

"얇은 밀가루 반죽 속에 수프를 넣고 오븐에 구운 요리야. 가리비나 랍스터 같은 해산물이 듬뿍 들어 있지. 노릇하게 구워진 빵을 포크로 찢고 여전히 바다 내음을 간직한 신선하고 뜨거운 수프의 향을 처음 맡는 순간을

Wharf. It was the clam chowder I had at the seafood restaurant on the beach. Clam chowder at Fisherman's Wharf on a rainy day. That was what I liked the most."

Jae-i watched him speak, a faraway look in his eyes. She had not expected him to say something like that. What people liked the most about their trips was a simple matter of preference—but no one ever mentioned something like clam chowder to a question asked in passing.

But then again, people didn't necessarily think of a Gothic cathedral's silhouette and its perfect beauty, or breathtaking scenery that would ordinarily elicit oohs and ahs. A yellow wild flower between old stonewalls that you ran into while walking through some nameless alley. The olive-colored tablecloth at a cafe you noticed only when the bus turned the corner. There were people who mentioned things like that, too.

"What's clam chowder?"

"It's a type of soup, cooked in an oven and served in a bread bowl. It's loaded with seafood, like scallops and lobster meat. The moment you tear off a piece of the bread bowl and breathe in the aroma of the fresh, hot soup that still smells

행복, 이라고 부를 수 있을까? 그래도 괜찮을 거 같아. 갈색이 도는 빵의 뚜껑을 터뜨릴 땐 정말 조심해야 해."

"왜요?"

"향에 매혹돼서 얼굴을 박고 있다가 구멍 사이로 터져 나오는 뜨거운 김에 코를 데거나 시력을 상실할 수 있어. 이게 그때 덴 자국이야."

남자는 코 옆의 한 곳을 손가락으로 짚으며 장난스럽게 웃는다. 오래된, 손톱 자국과 섞인 여드름 흉터다.

"우리 음식이 생각날 땐 그것보다 좋은 게 있어. 몽마르트르 언덕의 노천에서 파는 홍합요리도 괜찮아. 시원하고 담백한 국물 맛이 일품이거든. 요리라고 부르기엔 좀 그렇지? 싱싱한 홍합을 그냥 삶은 거니까. 여기서의 포장마차 홍합탕에 비해 비싸다 싶으면 입이 활짝 열린 걸로만 골라 반쯤 먹다 웨이터를 부르면 돼. 심각한 표정으로, 조개가 싱싱하지 않다고 클레임을 걸면 한 접시를 새로 받을 수 있지. 학교 다닐 때 먹다 남은 자장면에 미리 준비해간 파리를 한 마리 집어넣어 새로 한 그릇 얻어먹은 적이 있다면 아련한 추억에 젖게 되면서 즐거움은 두 배가 될 거야."

"해산물 요리를 좋아하나 봐요."

like the sea for the first time⋯ Happiness? Yes, I think you can say that's what you feel. When you tear through the top of the golden brown bread bowl, you have to be really careful."

"Why?"

"If you get so captivated by the aroma that you put your face too close to it, you might burn your nose from the hot steam bursting through the hole. You might even lose your eyesight. This is a scar I got from that."

He grinned mischievously as he pointed to the side of his nose. It was an old acne scar with fingernail marks.

"If you crave Korean food, then there's something better than that. The steamed mussels they sell at the outdoor restaurants at Montmartre are pretty good. The light broth is the best part. You can't call it a meal, I suppose, since it's just fresh steamed mussels. If you think it's too expensive compared to the steamed mussel soup you can get at the food stalls here in Korea, then after you eat about half of the mussels you should call the waiter. Then, you look serious and complain about how the mussels aren't fresh, and they'll give you a whole new plateful for free! If you've ever put a fly

남자는 길게 한숨을 쉬며 아련한 표정을 짓는다.

"그래. 해물요리라면 방콕의 허름한 야시장에서 먹은 볶음국수도 놓칠 수 없지. 죽순과 해산물을 넣어서 볶은. 돌아오는 길에 먹었던 여러 가지 곤충볶음의 고소함도 기억나는군."

"바퀴벌레?"

"글쎄. 그건 잘 모르겠고 메뚜기, 전갈, 매미, 뭐 그런 것들. 아, 선물 못 사와서 미안해. 일정이 너무 빡빡했고 동행이 있었어. 면세점에서까지 가이드를 해줘야 했지. 다음에 러시아 출장을 가게 되면 마트로시카를 사다줄게."

"그래요."

마트로시카라면, 재이의 서랍 속에도 한 세트가 들어 있다. 러시아가 아니라 동구의 어느 도시로 여행 갔던 친구가 사다준 것이다. 커다란 목각인형을 열면 똑같이 생긴, 조금씩 작은 사이즈의 인형들이 겹겹이 들어 있는 기념품. 재이는 마트로시카를 가지고 있다는 얘긴 하지 않는다. 말뿐, 이 사람은 선물 같은 걸 사다주는 성격은 아니니까.

"아니야. 재이한텐 그것보다 다른 선물이 어울려."

in your food at a Chinese restaurant when you were a kid, just so you could get a brand new bowl, it'll bring back your memories. And it'll be twice the fun."

"You must really like seafood."

He breathed a long sigh, and his eyes took on a dreamy look.

"Yes. When it comes to seafood, you can't forget about the stir-fry noodles from the humble night markets in Bangkok, with bamboo shoots and seafood. I also remember the savory stir-fried insects I had on the way back from the market."

"Roaches?"

"Hmm. I don't know if they had roaches, but I had grasshoppers, scorpions, cicadas, and things like that. Oh, I'm sorry I couldn't get you a present. I was on a tight schedule, and I had company. I had to guide him around even at the duty free shop. If I go to Russia for a business trip next time, I'll get you a Matryoshka doll."

"Okay."

Matryoshka doll. Jae-i already had a set sitting in her drawer. It was a gift from a friend who had been to some city in Eastern Europe, not Russia. A set of wooden dolls of decreasing size stored one

남자는 눈을 가늘게 뜨고 짧은 생각에 잠기는 척하더니 단정적으로 말한다.

"베니스에 가게 되면, 가면을 하나 사다주지. 산마르코 광장 옆, 곤돌라 선착장의 뒷골목으로 걸어가면 수백 년의 역사를 자랑하는 핸드메이드 가면을 취급하는 가게들이 있어. 공장에서 찍어낸 싸구려 가면과는 다른 느낌을 주지. 그걸 쓰면 정말 내가 다른 사람이 된 듯한? 뭐 그런 거야. 종이로 된 걸 원해? 아니면 석고?"

"석고는 좀 무거울 거 같네요."

"아무래도 그렇지? 클램차우더 수프라면 그곳보단 못하지만 괜찮게 하는 델 알고 있어. 내가 언제 한번 사주지."

그래요. 선선히 대답하지만 재이는 알고 있다. 이 남자와 굳이 바깥에서 만나는 일은 없을 것이다. 서로에게 필요한 건 이 작고 익숙한 공간 속에 모두 있다. 일주일에 한 번쯤 그가 여기로 와서 일용할 양식처럼 섹스를 하고 커피를 마시며 서로의 은닉된 삶의 한 조각씩을 이토록 풍요롭게, 이토록 인색하게 보여주는 것 이상은 원하는 게 없으니까.

"시차 때문에 피곤하겠다."

inside the other. Jae-i did not tell him that she already had a set. It was just all talk anyway. He wasn't the type to get her presents.

"Actually, I think a different gift would be better for you."

He knit his eyebrows slightly and narrowed his eyes, pretending to lose himself in thought for a bit.

"If I get to go to Venice, I'll bring you a mask," he said decidedly. "Near Piazza San Marco, in the back alley behind the gondola dock, there are shops that have been selling handmade masks for centuries. They feel very different from the cheap cookie-cutter masks they make in factories. When you put one on, you feel like a different person. Almost. You want one made out of paper? Or plaster?"

"Plaster would be pretty heavy."

"It would, wouldn't it? Oh, I know a restaurant that serves clam chowder, although it's not as good as the one at Fisherman's Wharf. I'll treat you sometime."

"Okay," Jae-i answered, but she knew that she wouldn't be seeing him outside of this building. All they needed from each other was here in this small, familiar space. Once a week or so, he came

"제트랙? 그런 건 내 사전에 없어."

후루룩 소리를 내며 커피를 마시는 동안만은 잠시 조용하다.

처음엔 지독히 수다스러운 남자를 보며, 재이는 그가 원하는 게 친밀함이라고 생각했다. 그리고 그의 의도는 성공하지 못할 거라는 냉정함으로 그를 지켜보았다. 수다가 두 사람을 가깝게 밀착시켜주는 건 아니다. 그런데, 어느 날 침을 튀기며 떠들어대는 그를 보며 재이는 자신이 잘못 알고 있다는 생각을 했다. 그가 수다스러운 건 결코 어느 선 이상으로 가까워지진 않겠다는 본능적인 거리두기인 것 같다는 그런 느낌. 어느 순간 말을 멈추고 싸늘히 식어버린 커피를 마시는 수그린 그의 이마에서 감추어진 피로의 자락이 얼핏 보이면, 커피를 마시기 전에 떠들었던 모든 말들이 사실은 무의미했음을 말없이, 그러나 완강하게 주장하는 것처럼 보였다.

보고 싶었어, 목소리를 낮추어 중얼거리며 코스요리의 마지막인 듯 남자는 재이의 머리카락을 어루만진다. 재이 역시 어쩐지 뜨거운 클램차우더 수프를 막 먹어치운 듯 나른해온다.

to her apartment to sleep with her, as if doing nothing more ordinary than eating his daily bread, and drank a cup of coffee; they shared small parts of their veiled lives in abundant, yet sparing detail. There was nothing more they wanted.

"You must be tired from jet lag."

"Jet lag? That's a word you only find in the dictionary of fools."

Then he became quiet as he slurped his coffee.

Because he was so chatty, Jae-i had thought he wanted intimacy at first. She'd coldly thought that there was no way he'd succeed in this, and so she'd begun to study him at a distance. Small talk would not narrow the distance between two people. But then, one day, as she watched him chatting away, she realized that she'd been mistaken all along. His endless chatter was his way of putting distance between the two of them, so as not to get closer to her beyond a certain extent. At some point, he would stop talking, and when she caught a glimpse of the exhaustion in his forehead as he stooped to drink his now cold coffee, it felt as if he was wordlessly and stubbornly asserting that everything he'd blabbered away about had all been meaningless.

I missed you, he murmured into her ear. He fon-

*

몇 개의 숫자를 눌러 현관문을 열고 들어설 때, 어둠
이 차갑고 커다란 손이 되어 온몸을 어루만지는 느낌이
싫다는 생각 같은 건 이제 하지 않는다. 시차 때문에 머
리는 멍했고 부족한 수면 상태에서 재이와 나누었던 섹
스의 피로는 묽은 커피 한잔으로는 가시지 않았다. 가
시지 않는 건, 육체의 피로만은 아닐 것이다. 재이에겐
출장이라고 했지만 휴가를 몰아서 샌프란시스코엘 다
녀왔다.

일주일 동안의 여행이 짧거나 혹은 아주 긴 한 편의
연극 같다는 생각이 그곳에 머무는 동안 머릿속에서 떠
나지 않았다. 한 편의 연극을 보러 그곳까지 간 건 아니
었다. 그러나 어쩐지 공항에 마중 나온 아내와 아이들
을 껴안는 순간부터, 자신이 우연히 공연을 보러갔다
무대 위의 누군가와 눈이 마주치고 그의 손에 이끌려나
가 물을 뒤집어쓴 채, 고소공포증이 극대화되는 높이에
서 외줄을 타며 입으로는 활짝 웃어야 하는, 즉흥공연
의 어리둥절한 관람객처럼 생각되었다.

공항의 환영객들 틈에 서 있던 아이들을 꼭 껴안던

dled her hair, as if it was the last course of a multi-course meal.

Jae-i also began to feel relaxed and drowsy, as if she'd just finished a warm bowl of clam chowder.

*

After pressing a few numbers on the keypad lock to open the door, I walked into the apartment. I no longer thought of how much I hated that feeling of darkness stroking my body like a huge, cold hand. I was lightheaded from jet lag, and a cup of weak coffee was not enough to fight my exhaustion from having sex with Jae-i. One weak cup of coffee wouldn't be enough to help even the smallest sense of my fatigue subside. And it probably wasn't just physical fatigue weighing me down. I'd told Jae-i that I had been on a business trip, but I had taken a short leave to go to San Francisco.

The whole time I was there, I couldn't help thinking constantly that this weeklong trip felt like a short—or, actually—a long play. I hadn't gone there to see some sort of play. But, for some reason, from the moment I hugged my wife and children at the airport, I felt like a bewildered spectator who'd

21

순간 등 뒤에 서 있던 아내가 지독히 낯설어 보였던 건 너무 노랗게 물들인 머리카락 때문이었을 것이다. 하지만 색색깔의 아트지로 'I LOVE YOU DADDY'라고 장식해놓았던, 작지만 온기 가득한 그 아파트에서 지낸 며칠 내내 누군가가 캠코더로 찍고 있기라도 하듯 행동한 것 같다는 느낌을 가진 건 지나친 예민함 때문이었을까.

처음, 아내가 아이들을 데리고 육 개월쯤 친정오빠가 있는 샌프란시스코에 가 있겠다고 했을 때만도 체류가 이렇게 길어질 줄은 몰랐다. 연년생인 오누이는 저희들끼리라도 삼촌네 보내달라고 옆에서 졸라댔다. 방학 한 달 연수로는 아무 효과가 없다고, 공부가 더 힘들어지기 전에 한 학기 동안만 다녀오겠다는 아내의 말에 생각해보자며 몇 달을 뭉그적거렸다. 그러다가 모든 사소한 문제들을 접고 보내기로 마음먹은 건 두 해 전 어느 일요일 오전이었다.

늦은 아침을 먹고 식탁에서 주간지를 읽고 있는데 아내가 금방 갈아서 뽑은 블루마운틴 커피를 들고 와 맞은편에 앉았다. 커피 맛은 더할 나위 없이 훌륭했다.

당신 커피는 예술이야.

gone to see an improv performance by chance, had caught the eyes of a performer and gotten pulled onto the stage, soaked in water from one of their gag spray guns, and made to walk on a tightrope at a height that maximized one's acrophobia, enduring this entire affair while smiling the whole time.

The reason my wife felt like a complete stranger to me as she stood behind the children I caressed there at the airport was probably her hair, dyed blonde. Too blonde. The days I spent in our small, but cozy apartment where the children had hung I LOVE YOU DADDY with construction paper, I felt like she was acting as if someone was recording us with a video camera. Was I being too sensitive?

At first, when my wife told me that she was going to take the children to San Francisco and stay with her brother for six months, I had no idea that things would drag on this long. My children, each only a year apart, had nagged at me to send them to their uncle's, even by themselves. When my wife told me that just a month of language study was not enough, that she would take them for a semester before their curriculum got even more difficult, I said I'd think about it and then let a few

의례적인 짧은 미소를 띠며 아내는 말했다.

애들 방학 시작하면 바로 떠날 거야.

어딜?

육 개월만 다녀올게. 애들도 애들이고.

멜로드라마에서 곤란한 얘기를 꺼내기 전에 사람들이 그러는 것처럼 아내도 말을 끊고 커피를 한 모금 마셨다.

애들도 애들이지만, 더 이상 견딜 수 없어.

입에 커피가 들어 있지 않았다면 뭐? 하고 되물었을 것이다. 아내와 같이 있는 시간이면, 모든 게 연극처럼 느껴지는 건 그때부터였던 것 같다. 나는 아내의 눈을 바라보았다. 아내도 시선을 피하지 않았다.

말해야 할 것 같아. 당신을 견딜 수 없어. 모든 걸. 국을 떠먹는 모습도, 수그린 머리의 가르마도, 웃는 모습도, 잠든 모습도, 엎드려서 신문을 들여다보는 것도, 그 모든 게. 당신을 보고 있으면 나라는 여자와 살고 있는 당신이 불쌍하다는 생각이 들어. 그 기분도 이젠 참을 수가 없어.

실내에 브람스가 흐르고 있는 걸 문득 깨달았다. 음악이 없었다면 그 침묵의 무게를 어떻게 견뎌냈을까. 나

more months slip by. Then, one Sunday morning, I finally decided to put aside all the trivial reasons and send them away. That was two years ago.

I'd been sitting at the table after a late breakfast, reading a weekly magazine, when my wife brought a Blue Mountain coffee she'd just brewed and sat down across from me. The coffee tasted absolutely wonderful.

Your coffee is perfect.

She smiled courteously and said, *We'll be leaving as soon as summer vacation starts for the kids.*

Leaving for where?

We'll just be gone for six months. The kids want to go too.

Just like the people in TV dramas before they bring up an awkward topic, my wife stopped talking and took a sip of her coffee.

The kids want to go too, and I can't stand it anymore.

If my mouth had not been full of coffee, I probably would have spat out, *What?* right there. I think it was from that moment on that I felt like I was in some sort of play whenever I was with my wife. I looked her in the eyes. She didn't look away.

I think I have to tell you. I can't stand you anymore. Everything. The way you eat your soup, the part in your hair

는 아내의 고백을 심각하게 받아들였다. 술을 마시고 아무 데나 토한 거라든가, 새로 산 린넨 시트에 담뱃재를 떨어뜨린 일이라든가, 아내의 배 위에서 트림을 한 일, 또 함부로 방귀를 뀌는 따위의, 아내가 늘 화를 내던 일에 대해 못 견디겠다 했다면 그토록 심각하진 않았을 것이다. 그런데 가르마라니, 내가 웃고 있을 때조차 마음속으로는 견딜 수 없어, 중얼거렸다니. 아내의 갑작스런 그 말은 충격이었다. 아내가 견딜 수 없다는 점들은 모두 변경될 수 없는 것들이었다. 아내가 견딜 수 없다는 것은 결국 나 자신이었다. 방법은 한 가지뿐이었다. 헤어져 지내는 시간. 그렇게 생각하자 육 개월 간의 별거야말로 두 사람에게 가장 필요한 것처럼 절실해졌다.

나를 똑바로 쳐다보며 견딜 수 없다고 말하는 아내의 입술을 바라보며, 커피를 마지막 한 방울까지 마셨다. 끝없이 변화하는 것들로 이루어진 삶 속에서 절대 변하지 않을 굳건한 어떤 것들의 범주에 속한다고 믿었던 것이 한순간 뒤틀리는 순간, 내 껍데기의 표정만이라도 굳세게 붙들고 있어야 했다. 나는 이후로 다시는 브람스를 듣지 않았다.

무심코 웃다가 아내가 했던 말이 떠오르기도 했지만

I see when you bend your head, the way you laugh, the way you sleep, the way you read your newspaper lying on your belly. Everything. When I look at you, I feel awful that you're living with a woman like me. And I can't stand that anymore either.

I suddenly realized that Brahms was playing in the living room. I don't know how I could have endured the silence if there'd been no music. I took her words seriously. I might have taken them less seriously if she'd told me that she couldn't stand me for all the things that had always made her angry, like the time I came home drunk and vomited inside the house, or the time I let cigarette ashes fall on the new linen, or when I'd burped while lying on top of her, or for farting anywhere, any time. But the part in my hair? She was thinking about how she couldn't stand me even when I laughed?

I was shocked. Everything my wife could not stand about me was things that I couldn't change. What she couldn't stand was, in fact, me. There was only one solution. Spending time apart. When I thought about that, six months of separation seemed like something we both desperately needed.

십 년 이상을 한 공간에서 부대끼고도 가르마가 보기 싫어지지 않는다면 그것도 이상하지 않은가 생각할 만큼 나는 아내를 이해하려 애를 썼다.

아이들은 메일을 보내왔다. 아빠, 한 달이나 아빠를 못 보다니. 메일은 자주 왔다. 두 달이나 아빠를 못 보았어. 또 메일이 왔다. 아아, 세 달이나 아빠를 못 보다니, 만나면 꼭 안아줄 거야. 그 다음부턴 아이들은 날짜를 세지 않았다. 언제부턴가 메일의 끝에 아이들은 낯선 이름을 적어놓기 시작했다. 아들은 마이클, 딸년은 에밀리. 운전을 하다, 서류를 검토하다, 마이클, 에밀리, 틈틈이 중얼거리며 나는 아이들의 얼굴과 그 이름을 연결해보곤 했다.

지나고 보니 육 개월은 금방이었다. 아내는 전화로 말했다. 일 년은 채워야 될 거 같아. 이제야 아이들이 친구들과 떠듬떠듬 대화를 나누기 시작해. 지금 돌아가긴 너무 아까워. 식사 잘 챙겨. 굶지 말고.

엄마의 말을 증명하듯 그날 마이클의 메일엔 그렇게 적혀 있었다. 아빠, 오늘은 친구 녀석과 싸웠는데 영어가 막 나오는 거 있지. 전엔 버벅거리다가 화가 나면 나도 모르게 한국말로 욕했거든. 야 이 새끼야. 근데 오늘

As I watched her lips move as she faced me directly and said she couldn't stand me, I gulped down the last drops of my coffee. In that moment, what I once believed were things that would never change in my life, which were, in fact, composed of ever-changing things, suddenly all warped and distorted. At the very least, I had to maintain the expression on my face. Since then, I've never listened to Brahms.

At times when I laugh, I'm reminded of what my wife said, but I try to understand her: maybe not growing to hate the part in my hair after living for over ten years together would be just as strange.

My children sent me emails. *Dad, I can't believe I haven't seen you for a month.* Their emails came frequently. *We haven't seen you for two months.* Another email: *Goodness, I haven't seen you for three whole months. When I see you, I'm going to give you a big hug.* After that email, they stopped counting the days.

Then they started to sign strange names at the end of the emails. My son wrote Michael, and my daughter, Emily. While driving, or reviewing some documents, I chewed over their names, Michael and Emily, and tried to link their faces to their new names.

은 신나서 마구 싸웠어. 요즘 우리 학교 매점엔 떡볶이 가 새로운 메뉴로 등장했어. 한국에서 먹는 것처럼 맵 진 않은데 나도 이젠 이게 더 맛있어. Daddy I miss you. 마지막 문장을 보자 케첩으로 색깔을 냈다는 떡볶 이의 맛을 짐작할 수 있을 것 같았다.

이번에 갔던 건, 세 사람이 잘 지내는지 보러 간 게 아 니라 이제 그만 귀국하기를 설득하려는 것이었다. 코를 델 듯 뜨거운 클램차우더 수프 같은 건 없었다. 그날 넷 이서 피셔먼스워프에 갔을 땐 너무 햇살이 따갑고 건조 해서 소나기라도 왔으면 좋겠다는 생각을 했을 뿐이다. 바닷가에 죽 늘어선 가게에서 찐 게를 사 먹었다. 치과 도구처럼 생긴 길고 날렵한 기구로 게살을 파먹으면서 도 나는 계속 누군가가 그 장면을 촬영하고 있는 것처 럼 얼굴 근육이 뻣뻣했다. 금문교 아래를 오가는 유람 선을 타자는 아이들에게는 비행기 멀미가 아직 가라앉 지 않았다며 엄살을 부렸다. 집요한 햇살 때문인지, 아 내는 서투른 치과기공사처럼 손을 움직이면서도 선글 라스를 벗지 않았다. 선글라스를 쓴 채 게를 파먹는 아 내가 컬트영화의 주인공처럼 보였다. 선글라스를 쓰고 화장실에 앉아 있는. 햇살은 살갗에 가벼운 통증을 유

In retrospect, the six months flew by. *I think we should stay for at least a year*, my wife said over the phone. *They've just begun to talk to their friends in broken English. It would be a waste to go back now. Make sure you eat well. Don't skip meals.*

As if backing up his mother, Michael also emailed me:

Dad, I was arguing with a friend today, and I was blurting things out in English. Before, I'd get all tongue-tied and end up cursing in Korean when I got angry. You little shit! But I was all excited today, and I argued with him. At our school, we now get tteokboki too. It's not as spicy as the ones in Korea, but now I like it more. Daddy I miss you.

I looked at the last sentence, written in English, and thought that I could taste the ketchup *tteokboki* in my mouth.

The reason I went this time was not to see if the three of them were doing well but to persuade them to come home. There was no clam chowder, hot enough to burn my nose. The day the four of us went to Fisherman's Wharf, I only wished for rain because the sunlight on my skin felt too hot and dry. We had steamed crabs at one of the restaurants along the beach. Even when I dug into the

31

발했지만 모든 게 비현실적으로 느껴지는 게 햇살 때문은 아니었다. 재이에게 입에서 나오는 대로 떠들고 났을 땐 진짜 비 내리는 피셔먼스워프에서 클램차우더 수프를 먹었던 게 아닐까 하는 생각이 들기도 했다.

그곳으로 가기 전 마지막 받은 이메일에 딸아이는 그렇게 써놓았다. 아빠가 여기 와서 같이 살면 안 돼? 샌드위치 가게를 하든 야채장사를 하든. 난 돌아가고 싶지 않아. 엄마와 오빠가 꼭 돌아가야 한다면 난 혼자서라도 여기 남아 있을 거야. 아빠가 보고 싶긴 하지만 죽어도 돌아가지 않을 거야. 죽어도, 라는 단어는 열한 살짜리가 내뱉을 말은 아니었다. 메일을 보낸 건 딸아이지만 그 메일 속엔 세 사람의 목소리가 뒤섞여 메아리쳤다.

배가 고프다. 빈속에 커피 한 잔 마신 게 전부니. 오래전부터 냉장고 속은 텅 비어 있다. 라면을 끓여서 냄비째 들고 와 바닥에 신문을 깔아 올려놓고 자정뉴스를 보며 먹었다. 김치라도 있으면 좋겠는데. 국물을 마시려고 보니 개미 한 마리가 동동 떠 있다. 젓가락으로 건져 신문지에 털어내고 냄비를 들어 올리니 신문지가 들러붙어 따라온다. 라면국물 얼룩진 신문에는, 화물선의

crab with the long, agile tool that looked like something you'd find at the dentist's, my face felt tense and stiff as if I was being filmed. The children wanted to go on the boat that cruised under the Golden Gate Bridge, but I turned them down, saying that I still hadn't gotten over my airsickness.

Maybe it was because of the sunlight burning insistently down on us all day that my wife never took off her sunglasses, even as she dug into her crab and fumbled away like an amateur dental technician. In her sunglasses and with her hands full of crab, my wife looked like a heroine out of some cult film. A heroine wearing sunglasses while sitting on a toilet. The sunlight pierced and pricked at my skin—but the sunlight wasn't the only reason I felt as if everything was unreal. After I'd babbled to Jae-i, saying whatever had come into my mind, I actually began to wonder whether I really had had a bowl of clam chowder at Fisherman's Wharf that rainy day.

In the last email I received from my daughter before I went to San Francisco, she wrote:

Dad, can't you come here and live with us? You can run a deli or a grocery store. I don't want to go back to Korea. If mom and Michael have to go back, I'm going to

창고에 숨어 영국으로 밀입국하려던 중국인 29명이 고온과 산소 부족으로 전원 사망한 외신이 짤막하게 적혀 있다. 냄비를 든 채 그 기사를 가만히 들여다보았다. 죽어도, 라는 딸아이의 목소리가 라면국물처럼 신문지에 배어 있다. 미지근해진 국물을 마저 마시고 말끔히 설거지를 했다.

돌아오자는 말은 끝내 하지 못했다. 목숨을 걸고 밀입국하려던 중국인들처럼, 아내는 여기만 아니면 그곳이 어디든 상관없는 것처럼 보였고 아이들에게 그곳은 좀 더 일찍 발견하지 못한 게 한스러운 낙원이었다.

*

퇴근하면 습관처럼 켜놓기만 할 뿐 잘 보지는 않는 텔레비전 앞으로 재이를 부른 건 낯익은 음색과 억양의 목소리다. 프라이팬에 찬밥을 볶다 마루로 달려 나갔다. 위층 남자다. 비오는 퍼셔먼스워프에서 먹었던 클램차우더 수프가 가장 좋았다던.

화면 아래쪽의 제목은 '자발적인 이산, 기러기아빠'다. 기러기아빠? 재이로선 약간 놀랍긴 했지만 충격적일

stay here even if it's all by myself. I miss you, Daddy, but I'm not going back even if it kills me.

"Even if it kills me" was not a phrase that an eleven-year-old would use. Although the email had been from my daughter, I could hear the voices of all three of them echoing throughout that email.

I felt hungry. No wonder, since I'd only had a cup of coffee on an empty stomach. The refrigerator had been empty for some time. I made instant noodles, placed the pot on an old newspaper, and ate while watching the midnight news. It would've been nice if there was some *kimchi*. When I held up the pot to drink the broth, I saw a dead ant floating inside. I fished it out with my chopsticks and picked up the pot again, and this time, the newspaper stuck to the bottom of the pot came up too. There was a short article on the first page of the stained newspaper about 29 Chinese people who had died from high temperature and lack of oxygen while trying to smuggle themselves into England. They'd been hiding in a container on a cargo ship.

I held the pot and stared at the article. My daughter's voice—"even if it kills me"—seemed to soak through the newspaper like the instant noodle

것까진 없었다. 가족관계에 대해선 물어본 적이 없으니. 벗은 등을 어루만지던 남자를 화면에서 보자니 이전에 실제로 가보았던 여행지를 텔레비전으로 보는 것 같은 그런 기분이 든다. 에로스와 우정을 오가는 듯한 이런 관계에서 중요한 건 질문을 하지 않는 거라는 걸 재이는 알고 있다. 너무 많은 걸 알려 하면 관계는 삐걱거리기 시작한다. 질문하지 않았으므로 그는 대답하지 않았을 뿐이다. 자작거리는 소리가 나며 밥 눋는 냄새가 난다. 부엌으로 달려가 프라이팬을 들고 와 바닥에 앉는다. 그는 푸른 폴로 셔츠를 입고 있다. 화면 속에서도 그는 여전히 수다스러웠으며 몇 번인가 환하고 보기 좋게 웃는다.

물론 외롭죠. 빈방들 틈에서 불 꺼진 거실로 들어서는 게 싫어서 살던 집은 세주고 원룸으로 옮겼어요.

재이는 옷을 입은 것보다 알몸이 더 익숙한 남자를 순간 낯설게 바라보았다. 다만 외로움 때문에 살던 아파트를 두고 좁은 원룸으로 옮겼다는 남자는 쿨해 보인다. 그가 외롭지 않았다면 이 원룸 빌딩의 엘리베이터에서 우리가 만날 일도 없을 것이니.

괜찮아요. 사랑하니까 감수하는 거죠. 무얼 위해서 이

soup. I finished off the lukewarm soup and did the dishes.

I was unable to tell them that we should all go back together. Just like the Chinese people who'd attempted to smuggle themselves into England at the risk of their lives, it seemed that my wife was fine if she could be anywhere but back home. And for the children, America was a paradise. Their only regret was not having discovered it sooner.

*

A familiar voice drew Jae-i to the TV, which she tended to turn on when she came home from work but didn't usually watch. She was in the middle of stir-frying rice in a pan when she heard him and rushed out into the living room. There he was right there on the television screen. It was the man from the upstairs. The man who had said he liked the clam chowder at Fisherman's Wharf the most.

On the bottom, a caption read "Voluntary Separation, Goose Fathers." Goose Fathers? Jae-i was slightly taken aback, but she wasn't shocked either. She had never asked him about his family. Now seeing him, whose naked back she'd often stroked,

렇게 헤어져 살아야 하나, 싶다가도 한 번씩 가보면 자식이라도 이런 환경에서 교육을 받게 하고 싶다는 생각이 절로 들어요. 돈이 있어도 여기선 누릴 수 없는 것들, 승마라든가 강변을 따라 흘러가는 조정 같은 정말 좋은 프로그램이 많죠. 여기 과외비 생각하면 학비가 그렇게 비싼 것도 아니구요.

재이는 들고 있던 숟가락에서 굳은 밥풀을 하나씩 떼어먹는다. 하긴 요즘 다 큰 자식과 와이프 끼고 사는 사내들은 모자라는 인간으로 보인다지. 텔레비전에 출연해서 눈물 한 방울 섞어 저렇게 말하는 걸 보니 내 집에서 볼 때보다 각이 나온다. 애들도 보고 싶고 집사람 없으니 사는 게 아니죠. 언제 시간 내서 아이들한테 가서 아버지 노릇도 하고 싶어요. 쿨한 남자답지 않게 화면 속의 그는 미간에 약간의 끈적이는 감정을 드러내며 고개를 떨군다. 가장 외로울 때요? 늘 사무친 정서인 듯 그의 대답은 금방 나온다. 안방불을 켜기도 전에 현관등이 꺼질 때, 혼자 밥 먹을 때, 누군가의 목소리가 그리워 보지도 않는 텔레비를 늘 켜놓은 자신을 보면서, 서랍에서 아내의 속옷을 보았을 때⋯⋯. 사랑이요? 아이들 때문에 헤어져 있긴 하지만 아내는 날 너무나 사랑

felt like seeing a place she'd been to on TV. Jae-i knew that not asking questions was important in their sort of relationship, which swung between sex and friendship. If they try to learn more about each other, their relationship would start to give in. Since she hadn't asked, he'd just never answered. The sizzling sound and the smell of charred rice wafted out of the kitchen. She ran into the kitchen and brought out the frying pan and sat on the living room floor. He was wearing a blue polo shirt. He was chatty even on the screen, and a few times he smiled, looking bright and attractive.

"Of course I'm lonely. I hated the feeling of walking into a dark living room surrounded by empty rooms, so I rented out my old apartment and moved into a studio."

Momentarily, the man whose naked body was more familiar to her felt like a stranger. The man, who'd said he left his apartment and moved into a small studio just because he was lonely, seemed distant. If he had not been lonely, they would not have met in the elevator of this studio apartment building.

"It's okay though. Love makes everything possible. At certain times, I wonder why we are living

하죠. 모르겠어요. 언제까지 헤어져 있을 진.

그가 거짓말을 했다고는 생각지 않는다. 다만 말하지 않았을 뿐이다. 재이 역시, 그에게 일상의 모든 걸 말해주는 건 아니니까. 그러니 배신감 같은 걸 느낄 이유도 없다. 그의 감추인 부분을 끝내 모르는 채로, 그리고 모르는 체하며 살고 싶다. 너의 외로움이나 공허감까지 같이 껴안기엔 내 몫만도 너무 무겁다. 과장된 것처럼 보이는 그의 쾌활함, 밝음, 듣는 사람을 기어이 웃게 만드는 지독한 현학 취미. 더 이상 부족함이 없다.

샤워를 하고 잠자리에 들어 깜빡 잠이 들었나보다. 휴대폰이 울렸다.

나야. 커피 마시러 가도 돼?

여기, 병원이에요.

그래? 조용하네?

그럴 시간이잖아요.

귀찮은 환자들에게 수면제를 주사했군. 그렇지? 다음엔 케타민 앰플을 하나씩 주사해줘.

케타민?

악몽을 꾸게 하는 약물이지. 끈끈하고 진저리나는 악몽과 불쾌한 환각에 시달리게 하는 마취제야. 그 주사

apart like this. But when I actually go and see my family, I can't help think that I'd love to have my children live and learn in an environment like this. There are a lot of programs for activities we don't even have here, even if you had the money. Like horseback riding or crew. Plus, if you think about all the money that goes into private education here, the tuition there isn't all that expensive."

One by one, Jae-i picked out the grains of rice stuck on her spoon. Well, people did say that nowadays men who live with their wives and grown up children were ludicrous. But he did look much more attractive now on TV than he did in her apartment, talking and his eyes full of tears.

"I miss my children and, since my wife's not home... it's not a great life for me. I want to take some time off and go see my children, and actually spend some time with them."

Unlike his usual aloof self, he dropped his head slightly and a sappy sort of look flashed across his face.

"When do I feel most lonely?"

As if it had been buried in his heart for a long time now, he answered right away.

"When the motion sensor light in my entranceway

를 맞고 잠들었다 깨어나면 자신이 누워 있는 병실이 얼마나 평온하며 따스한 곳인지 뼈저리게 깨닫게 될 거야. 불친절하네 어쩌네 불평 따윈 안 할 거라구.

그럴게요. 케타민.

거짓말을 하고 싶진 않은데 오늘은 만나고 싶지 않다. 다국적 제약회사에 근무하며 한 달에 한 번 꼴로 해외 출장을 간다고 말했지만 이번 여행은 개인적 여행이었을 것이다. 그는 샌프란시스코를 다녀왔다고 말했고, 그의 가족이 있는 곳은 샌프란시스코라고 텔레비전에서 말했다. 혹은 출장길에 가족을 만나고 왔을 수도 있을 것이다. 그렇게 궁금하지도 않다. 살짝 궁금한 건 그의 아내의 얼굴이었는데 프로그램이 끝날 때까지 그 여자는 나오지 않았다. 끔찍이 남편을 사랑하지만 아이들 때문에 샌프란시스코에 가 있다는 그 여자는. 제약회사에 다닌다는 말은 사실일까. 케타민은, 사람에게 쓰는 마취제는 아니다.

*

재이는 지금 집에 있을 것이다. 너무 가까이 사는 게

turns off automatically, even before I can turn the light on in my room. When I am eating alone. When I see myself turning on the TV that I don't even watch only because I miss hearing someone's voice. Or when I see my wife's underwear in my drawers... Love? Of course, my wife loves me, even though we are living apart for our children's sake. I'm not sure when this will come to a close."

Jae-i didn't think he lied to her. He just didn't tell her everything. It wasn't like Jae-i told him everything about herself. So she had no reason to feel betrayed. She wanted to live on without knowing, pretending as if she knew nothing about the life he wanted to keep from her. My own burden is too heavy for me to embrace your loneliness and emptiness. His seemingly exaggerated glee and liveliness, and his pedantic jokes that always ended up making her laugh. There was nothing more she needed.

She must have fallen asleep in her bed right after taking a shower. Her phone was ringing.

"It's me. Can I come over for a cup of coffee?"

"I'm at the hospital."

"Really? It's so quiet."

"It's about time."

43

좋지 않은 건 이럴 때이다. 늦게 들어오면서 올려다본 그녀의 창엔 불이 켜져 있었다. 하긴 오늘은 보고 싶지 않아, 라는 말을 듣는 것보단 병원이라고 거짓말하는 게 나을지도 모른다. 보고 싶지 않다거나 당신을 견딜 수 없다는 말을 대놓고 한다는 건, 말하는 사람이 짐작하는 것보다 훨씬 더 가혹한 폭력이다.

퇴근하면서 들른 할인점에서 쇼핑을 하면서 예전처럼 보이는 것마다 이것저것 집어서 카트에 담진 않았다. 다섯 개씩 묶인 라면도 가격을 세심히 비교하며 골랐다. 식품 코너에선 취향보다는 덤이 붙은 것을 집는 게 습관이 되었다. 살던 아파트를 세를 주고 지금 살고 있는 원룸을 얻고 나서 은행에 넣어둔 여유돈은 눈에 뜨이게 줄어들었다.

샌프란시스코에 가면 오빠네 있다 올 거야, 했던 아내는 한 달도 안 돼서 오빠 집을 나왔다. 세 가지 이유를 들면서. 올케 눈치가 보인다는 것과 사촌들 사이의 미묘한 감정대립에서 아이들을 기죽이고 싶지 않다는 것, 그리고 아이들이 사촌들과 한국말만 해서 도대체 왜 여기 왔는지 모를 지경이라는 것. 세 가지 전부, 가르마나 웃는 모습처럼 내가 어찌할 수 없는 것들이었다. 그곳

"You gave sleeping drugs to the annoying patients, didn't you? Next time, you should give them each a shot of ketamine."

"Ketamine?"

"It's a nightmare inducing drug. It's an anesthetic that makes people have awful nightmares and hallucinations. When they wake up, they'll be painfully aware of how peaceful and warm the hospital room is. They won't ever be able to complain about how unfriendly the nurses are, you know."

"I'll keep that in mind. Ketamine."

She didn't want to lie, but she didn't want to see him today. He said he worked for a multinational pharmaceutical company and had to go on business trips once a month or so. But this one probably had been a personal trip. He told her he went to San Francisco. He said his family was in San Francisco on TV. He might have met up with them on the way back from his business trip. She wasn't even that curious. She was slightly curious about what his wife looked like, but she never appeared on the show. That woman who adored her husband but was in San Francisco for their children. She wondered if it was true that he worked at a pharmaceutical company. Ketamine was not an an-

의 집세는 테헤란로 임대료 뺨쳤고 게다가 월세였다.

처음 혼자 지내게 됐을 땐 그래도 자신이 그 생활을 약간은 즐겼었다는 생각이 든다. 가끔 나이트클럽에 들렀고 스물 몇 살짜리 여자애들과 술을 마시고 함께 자는 건 어렵지 않았지만 모텔에 갔을 때의 비용이 부담스럽게 느껴지기 시작했다. 무엇보다도 섹스가 끝난 후면 지루한 고깃덩어리처럼 느껴지기 시작하는 낯선 여자와, 깨고 싶은 연대감 속에서 모텔의 복도가 너무 길다는 생각을 하며 걸어 나오는 일도 점점 지겨워졌다. 지하주차장이나 자동차극장에서 카섹스를 해본 적도 있다. 모텔이란 데가 그래. 몰래카메라에 찍혀 졸지에 포르노배우로 데뷔하고 싶진 않아, 말했지만 그때도 은행잔고를 생각하지 않을 수가 없었다. 차에서 하면 더 흥분된다는 건 사실이 아니다. 호기심으로 한번 해보는 게 아니면 좁고 불편하고 끊임없이 바깥에 신경이 쓰일 뿐이다.

재이를 만나기 전까지 그런 생활을 꽤 오래 했다.

토요일 오전이었다. 집 근처의 마켓에서 몇 가지 생필품을 고를 때 스쳤던 재이를 다시 엘리베이터 앞에서 마주치자 나는 약간 웃으며 목례를 했다. 둘이서만 엘

esthetic you would use on people.

*

Jae-i was probably home. At times like these, living within such close proximity wasn't so great.
When I looked up at the building on the way home,
the light was on in Jae-i's apartment. But then,
maybe it was better to hear her lie and say that she
was at the hospital instead of saying that she didn't
want to see me. Saying things like "I don't want to
see you" or "I can't stand you" to someone's face
was an even more cruel violence than the speaker
could assume.

At the discount store I stopped by on the way
home from work, I didn't put just anything in the
cart like I used to. I checked and compared the
prices of bundles of instant noodles before choos-
ing one. In the food section, I grew accustomed to
buying stuff with freebies instead of ones I like. After I rented out my apartment and moved into the
studio apartment, my bank account shrank notice-
ably.

We'll stay at my brother's place in San Francisco, my
wife had said. But in less than a month she'd left.

리베이터를 탄 적도 있고 다른 사람들과 섞여 탄 적도 있었다. 늘 혼자였다. 혼자 살면서 연인도 없는 싱글들에게 토요일은 삶이 파삭거리는 모래처럼 발가락 사이로 흘러내리는 시간이다. 아무래도 일 년은 채워야겠어, 아내가 그렇게 통보했을 무렵이었다. 숫자판에 눈을 준 채 물어보았다.

영화 보러 가실래요? 티켓이 있는데.

티켓이 있다는 건 사실이 아니었다. 좋아하는 감독의 특별영화제가 끝나가고 있었는데 대중성 있는 영화가 아니라 표는 언제라도 살 수 있을 것이었다. 여자가 대답도 하기 전에 엘리베이터는 칠 층에 멈추었다.

아니에요.

여자는 거절한 게 미안한 듯 살짝 웃으며 내렸다. 그래서였을 것이다. 열림 버튼을 누른 채 빠르게 말했다.

놓치면 후회할 영화예요. 한 시간 후에 현관 앞에서 봐요.

대답을 듣지 않고 버튼에서 손을 뗐다. 여자의 입이 약간 벌어졌다. 혼자 살면서 늘어난 건 여자에게 작업할 때의 순발력뿐이다. 여자는 열두 시가 조금 지나서 내려왔다. 샤워를 했는지 아까와 달리 씻은 배추처럼

She'd left for three reasons. She felt uncomfortable because of her sister-in-law. She didn't want the children to feel discouraged in their subtle emotional confrontations with their cousins. And the children hung out with their cousins all day, speaking Korean, so it didn't feel like they were in the US. Just like the part in my hair or the way I laugh, there was nothing I could do to change those three things. The rent there was as expensive as an apartment would be in Gangnam, and they had to pay it every month on top of that.

For the first few weeks since I began to live alone, I think I enjoyed it a bit. I went to clubs a few times, and it wasn't hard to drink and sleep with girls in their twenties. But soon, the money I had to spend at motels began to weigh down on me. Above all, it grew tiresome to walk out of a motel with a strange woman who had begun to feel like a boring lump of meat, wanting to end this comradeship bound by sex and feeling like the hallway was too long. I'd also had car sex in an underground parking lot and in a drive-in theater.

Motels are a little iffy. I don't want to get caught on one of the hidden cameras and make my debut as a porn star, I told the women. But in fact, I couldn't help think-

파릇해져 있었다.

좀 자야 되는데. 퇴근하는 길이었거든요.

병원에서 근무하시죠?

어떻게 아세요?

귀 옆에 실핀이 꽂혀 있더군요. 너스캡을 보면 늘 그 걸로 고정돼 있던데요.

관찰력이 대단하시네요.

아무나 관찰하는 건 아닙니다.

실핀이 아니라 여자에게서 나던 설핏한 소독약 냄새 때문이었지만 낯선 여자 옆에서 코를 킁킁대는 남자로 보이고 싶진 않았다. 프랑스 영화가 대개 그렇듯 영화 는 공부하듯 보면 재미를 느낄 수도 있었겠지만 대체로 지루했다. 수면이 부족했는지, 여자는 중간에 내 어깨 에 머리를 기대고 잠시 졸았다. 젖내 같은 게 살짝 번졌 다. 나올 때 구내매점에서 OST 시디를 사서 여자에게 주었다. 복잡한 로비에 잠시 멈추어 서서 여자는 포스 터 속의 여자 얼굴을 쳐다보았다. 극장 근처에서 국물 이 지나치게 달콤한 일본 우동을 먹고 집으로 돌아왔 다. 차 안에서 여자가 물었다.

프랑스 영화를 좋아하세요?

ing about my bank account balance even then. It wasn't true that having sex in the car was more exciting, unless you were doing it out of curiosity for the first time. It's cramped, uncomfortable, and you constantly worry about someone passing by outside.

That was how I lived for some time. Then I met Jae-i.

It was a Saturday morning. I'd walked past her in the market near my apartment building when I went to pick up a few household items. Then, when I ran into her waiting for the elevator, I smiled a bit and gave her a courtesy nod. We'd taken the elevator just by ourselves and with other people before. She was always alone. For singles living alone, the hours on Saturdays feel like dry sand slipping between your toes. *I'm afraid that it looks like we'll have to be here for a year*, my wife had just notified me.

"Want to go see a movie? I have tickets," I asked her while staring at the buttons on the elevator.

It wasn't true that I had tickets. There was a special screening for a director I liked, but it wasn't a popular film so buying the tickets was not a problem. The elevator stopped on the seventh floor

그다지. 그냥 같이 영화를 보고 싶었을 뿐이에요.

여자는 시디를 꺼내 오디오에 넣었다. 생이 자신에게 던진 수수께끼를 이해할 수 없다는 표정으로 마켓에서 생필품을 사던 여주인공의 모습 위로 흐르던 음악이다. 이 음악이 흐를 때 내 어깨에 기대어 자고 있었는데.

멜로디가 슬프고도 아름답네요. 가사의 뜻이 뭐예요?

나도 불어는 몰라요. 아까 자막에선 그렇게 나오던데. ……여름의 끝이 이토록 아름다웠던 적은 없었네. 헤어지기에 이토록 아름다운 순간은 없었네…….

여자는 앞을 쳐다보며 나지막이 따라해 보았다.

여름의 끝이 이토록 아름다웠던 적은 없었네. 헤어지기에?

그새 잊었는지 질문하듯 나를 돌아보았다. 눈을 쳐다보며 한 번 더 일러주었다.

헤어지기에 이토록 아름다운 순간은 없었네.

고개를 끄덕이며 여자는 중얼거렸다.

헤어지기에 이토록 아름다운 순간은 없었네.

갑자기 둘이 오래된 연인처럼 느껴졌다. 서로에 대한 탐색의 열의가 사라진. 그 노래의 가사 때문이었을까. 이후의 우리 관계의 내면은 대체로 그러했던 것 같다.

before Jae-i answered.

"No thank you."

She walked out, smiling a little as if to apologize for her rejection. That was probably why. I pressed on the button to hold the elevator door open and I spoke fast.

"You'll regret it if you miss it. I'll see you at the front of the building in an hour."

I didn't wait for her answer and took my finger off the button. Her mouth was agape. The only thing that I was able to hone while living alone was my ability to seduce women. She came down a few minutes after noon. She must have taken a shower because she looked refreshed, like a head of lettuce soaked in water.

"I have to sleep a bit," she said. "I was on my way home from work." She smiled somewhat apologetically.

"You work at a hospital, right?"

"How'd you know?"

"You had a bobby pin above your ear. Nurses keep their caps fixed with those, I've noticed."

"You must be really observant."

"I don't observe just anyone."

It wasn't the bobby pin, but a faint smell of steril-

그건 장점이 많은 관계이다. 피곤한 집중 대신 느긋한 여유를 가질 수 있는. 날카로운 칼에 쓸데없이 마음을 찔릴 일은 없는.

*

"아, 정말 맛있다. 소설가 하루키는 뜨거운 우동 국물을 먹는 어느 순간에 바깥세상이야 어떻게 되든 상관없다는 생각이 든다는 고백을 했는데 말야. 이 김치찌개야말로 세상이 어떻게 돌아가든 상관없단 생각이 들게 하는데?"

자주는 아니지만 이 남자는 전화를 해서 뭔가가 먹고 싶다는 얘길 가끔 한다. 솔직히 귀찮다. 내가 지 마누라야. 김치찌개 해놓고 기다리게, 그런 생각이 들긴 하지만 특별한 비용이나 수고가 드는 요리를 원하는 것은 아니어서 대체로 들어주는 편이다. 이를테면 얼리지 않은 갈치를 붉은 고추를 듬뿍 다져 넣고 짜게 조린 것이라든지 새우두부찌개, 혹은 깻잎을 넣은 김치볶음 따위. 결코 요리를 잘하지 않는 재이가 해놓은 음식들을 호들갑스러운 감탄사를 연발하며 먹는 걸 보고 있노라

izer about her. But I did not want to look like a man who walks around, sniffing strange women.

Like most French films, the film might have been interesting if you were a film student. For the most part, it was boring. Possibly because she didn't get enough sleep, she leaned her head against my shoulder and dozed off for a bit during the movie. A faint baby smell wafted from her. On the way out, I bought the soundtrack for the film from the gift shop and gave it to her. In the crowded lobby, she stopped for a second to stare into the face of the woman in the movie poster. Afterward, we went to a Japanese restaurant near the theater and each had a bowl of *udon* with broth that tasted a little too sweet before returning home.

"You like French films?" She asked me when we got back to my car.

"Not really. I just wanted to watch a movie with you."

She took the CD out of the case and put it into the CD player. Music began to flow out of the speakers, the background music that played when the film's heroine, looking as if she had no idea how to answer life's riddles, picked items out at a market. Jae-i had fallen asleep on my shoulder this

55

면 얼핏 안쓰럽다는 생각이 스치기도 했다.

"작년 가을에 파리에 일주일간 출장을 갔는데 대학 동기가, 마침 비어 있는 제 친구네 아파트에 묵게 해주었어. 한기가 뼛속으로 스미는데 그렇게 라면이 먹고 싶을 수가 없더라구. 걔보고 야, 라면 몇 개 갖다줘, 전화했는데 응 해놓고는 올 때까지 모르는 척하는 거야. 라면 몇 개에 인간이 그렇게 분노할 수 있다는 걸 그때 알았어. 그래 이놈아 한국 가면 나는 박스로 사다놓고 먹을 거야, 이를 갈았지. 지금도 그 생각하면 열받아."

"깜박 잊어버렸겠지."

"아니야. 아까워서 안 줬을 거야."

"아침은 굶는 편?"

"그렇진 않아. 마늘냄새를 풍기면 안 되니까 영국식 아침식사를 하지. 바싹 구운 토스트 한쪽, 달걀프라이, 블루마운틴, 그리고 브람스."

"아침에 듣는 브람스는 어때요?"

"브람스는 그랬지. 고독하되 자유롭다고. 난, 고독해야만 자유로움을 느껴. 고독은 내 일상의 에너지야."

안방불을 켜기 전에 현관등이 꺼질 때, 혼자 밥 먹을 때, 누군가의 목소리가 그리워 보지도 않는 텔레비를

song had first played.

"The melody's so beautiful. And sad. What's the song about?"

"I don't know French. But I think the subtitles were something like... the end of summer had never been so beautiful. And no moment was more beautiful for us to part."

"The end of summer had never been so beautiful," she looked straight ahead and repeated after me. "And no moment was...?"

She turned to me, as if asking me for the lyrics she's just heard but had already forgotten.

I looked into her eyes and repeated the lyrics for her.

"And no moment was more beautiful for us to part."

"And no moment was more beautiful for us to part," she murmured, nodding.

All of a sudden, it felt as if we were old lovers. No longer passionate about exploring each other. I wondered if it was because of the lyrics of that song. Since then, our relationship stayed that way for the most part. It was a relationship with many advantages. A relationship where I could relax instead of being on my toes. Where my heart

늘 켜놓은 자신을 볼 때, 서랍에서 아내의 속옷을 보았을 때. 그의 수다 위로 또 다른 그의 목소리가 겹쳐진다. 식탁을 훔치고 재이는 커피포트에서 주전자를 뽑아 물고기 모양의 나무판 위에 내려놓았다.

"블루마운틴은 아니에요."

"초보들은 블루마운틴이 제일인 줄 알지. 세상에는 다양한 커피가 있어. 커피의 물질적인 분류에 대해 알고 싶어? 아니면 형이상학적인 분류?"

이 남자, 그냥 놔두면 한 시간도 좋을 것이다. 원래는 아라비아 최음제의 재료였다는 커피의 기원에서부터 알려지지 않은 그로테스크한 용도까지. 그것도 이미 두어 번씩 들은 것들.

"제일 맛있는 게 뭐예요?"

"제일 맛있는 커피. 그건 너무나 어려운 질문이야. 커피의 취향이란 이성에 대한 기호만큼 주관적이고 불합리하니까."

"가장 비싼 커피는?"

"기호식품을 가격으로 등급 매기는 건 개장수들이나 하는 짓이지. 하노이에 가게 되면 말야. 여우똥 커피란 걸 마셔봐."

wouldn't be pierced with a sharp knife.

*

"Ah, it's really good! The Japanese novelist Haruki said that when you're drinking hot *udon* noodle soup, at some point, what's happening in the world stops mattering. And you know, this *kimchi* stew makes me stop caring about whatever that's happening in the world."

Not often, but sometimes, he called her to say that he wanted to eat a certain dish. Honestly, it was annoying. Was she his wife or what? Why did she have to wait for him with a bowl of *kimchi* stew? But the food he usually wanted were things that didn't require special ingredients or extraneous efforts, things like hairtail boiled down in soy sauce and a tablespoonful of diced red pepper, tofu soup seasoned with salted shrimp, or stir-fried *kimchi* with sesame leaves. So she ended up cooking for him for the most part. Jae-i wasn't a great cook at all, but when she watched him devour the food she prepared, all the while making a fuss and praising her, she felt sorry for him.

"Last fall, I went to Paris on a business trip. One

"여우똥이라면 베트남어?"

"아니. 그야말로 여우의 배설물 속에서 골라낸 커피원두를 볶은 거야."

"왜 그게 맛있을까?"

"내 추측으로는."

그는 오래 생각해온 문제라도 되는 듯 심각한 표정을 짓는다.

"여우란 놈이 약아서 아주 잘 익은 원두만 골라서 먹기 때문이라는 게 하나의 추측이고 긴 소화기관을 지나면서 원두가 미묘한 화학적 성분 변화를 일으킨 때문일 수도 있어. 어쩌면 둘 다일 수도 있고. 어쨌거나 베트남에 가서 이 커피를 사려면 무조건 가장 비싼 걸 사도록 해. 요즘은 그놈들이 약아져서 무조건 포장지에 여우그림을 찍어놨거든."

말하는 품이 지난주에 하노이의 커피 박람회에 다녀오기라도 한 것 같다.

"더 비싼 게 있어. 수마트라의 고양이똥 커피. 이건 사향고양이 배설물에서 골라낸 거지. 이게 세상에서 제일 귀한 커피원두야. 파리에 갔을 땐데 채식주의자를 위한 레스토랑에서 마셔봤어. 알로에 칵테일과 장미꽃 샐러

of my friends from college let me stay at his friend's apartment because it was empty at the time. But the place was so cold I was freezing down to my bones, and I really craved some instant noodles. So I called my friend and said, 'Hey, get me some instant noodles.' He said he would, but he didn't get me any. That's when I realized that a man could get extremely upset about instant noodles. I ground my teeth, thinking, 'Fine, you jerk. When I get back to Korea, I'll buy a box of instant noodles and eat them all by myself.' It still makes me angry when I think about it."

"He must have just forgotten about it."

"No, he probably didn't want to waste one on me."

"You skip breakfast?"

"Not really. Since I can't let my breath smell like garlic, I usually have an English-style breakfast. A piece of toast, eggs sunny-side up, a cup of Blue Mountain coffee, and Brahms."

"How's listening to Brahms in the morning?"

"Brahms once said he was lonely yet free. I only feel free when I'm lonely. Loneliness is what drives my life."

When the motion sensor light in my entranceway turns

드도 거기서 처음 맛보았지. 환상적이더군."

"이상한 냄새가 나진 않았어요?"

"노."

단호한 그의 목소리를 듣자니 너무도 평범한 커피를 내놓은 게 미안해졌다.

똑같은 한 사람에게서 사람들은 제각기 다른 면을 볼 것이다. 누구는 그 사람의 맑은 눈빛을, 유난히 긴 팔다리를, 자잘한 주름으로 기억되는 웃음을, 혹은 돈을, 권력을, 숨겨진 냉혹함을 읽어낼 수도 있을 것이다. 재이가 그에게서 처음 본 건 외로움이었다. 엘리베이터의 열림 버튼을 누르고 영화 보러 가실래요? 물었을 때 아니라고 거절하지 못했던 건 그의 웃음 띤 눈빛 뒤의 선명한 외로움이었다. 이후로 그에게서 많은 다른 것들을 보게 되었지만 그를 생각할 때면 처음 보았던 순간의 외로움이 맨 먼저 떠올랐다. 다만 그 커피 찌꺼기 빛깔의 외로움 뒤에 이토록 현란한 지적 허영과, 포즈로서의 삶이 베일처럼 드리워져 있으리라고는 알지 못했다.

커피를 마시던 그가 갑자기 미간을 찌푸리며 고개를 숙인다.

"왜? 왜 그래요?"

off automatically, even before I can turn the light on in my room. When I am eating alone. When I see myself turning on the TV that I don't even watch, only because I miss hearing someone's voice. Or when I see my wife's underwear in my drawers. A different voice than the one she was familiar with played over his chatter.

After cleaning up the table, Jae-i took the pot from the coffeemaker and placed it on the fish-shaped coaster.

"Well, this isn't Blue Mountain."

"People who don't know much about coffee think that Blue Mountain is the best. There are lots of different types of coffee in this world. Which one do you want to learn about? The material kinds of coffee or the metaphysical kinds?"

This man. If you let him, he'd talk for an hour all by himself. From the origins of coffee—an ingredient for Arabian aphrodisiacs—to other unknown, more harrowing usages. She'd already heard this all two or three times before.

"Which one tastes the best?"

"The best tasting coffee. Now that's a really difficult question. Coffee preferences are as subjective and unreasonable as sexual attraction."

"The most expensive one then?"

고통을 참는 그의 표정은 낯설다. 가늘고 길게 숨을 내쉬고는 그가 물었다.

"여기가 아픈 건 왜지?"

손바닥으로 가슴을 짚고 있다.

"어떻게 아파요?"

"조이는 것 같기도 하고 뻐근하기도 하고 따끔거리는 것 같기도 해."

"언제부터?"

"두어 달 전에도 한 번 그랬었는데."

"검진 한번 받아봐요. 심장 때문일 수도 있고 위산이 식도 쪽으로 역류해도 비슷한 증상이 나타나니까."

"그래? 어떤 게 더 치명적이지?"

"물론 심장이지."

"그럼 그걸로 할래."

재미있는 농담이라도 한 듯 그는 갑자기 크게 웃어댄다. 이마에 엷게 땀이 밴 채로.

"Only dog traders grade preferential food by price. If you ever go to Hanoi, try fox-dung coffee."

"Fox Dung? Is it Vietnamese?"

"No, it's literally coffee beans harvested from a fox's fecal matter."

"I wonder why that tastes good."

"I think," he began, his face becoming serious as if he had thought about it for a long time. "Foxes are sly, so they only eat the ripest coffee beans. That's one of my theories, and the other one is, maybe because the beans go through a subtle chemical compositional change as they travel through the fox's lengthy digestive track. Or it could be both. Anyway, if you want to buy some in Vietnam, make sure you get the most expensive kind. The vendors have gotten sly, so now they just print pictures of foxes on all the bags."

From the way he talked, you would have thought that he'd been to a coffee exhibition in Hanoi last week.

"There's even more expensive coffee. Kopi luwak from Sumatra. Collected from the fecal matter of civets. That's the rarest kind of coffee bean in the world. I had some at a vegetarian restaurant in Par-

*

　현관 문틈으로 가는 불빛이 새어나온다. 아침에 나가
면서 불을 켜놓고 나온 모양이다. 문득 내 목소리가 귓
속에서 울린다. 안방등을 켜기 전에 현관등이 꺼질 때.
그 프로그램은 방영이나 했을까. 언제라고 날짜와 시간
을 얘기해주었는데 기억나지 않는다. 보고 싶지도 않고.
　재이의 집에서 커피를 마시고 있을 때 가슴이 심하게
아파왔다. 격통이었다. 통증을 참으며 미소를 짓는 건
쉽지 않았다. 한 번도 마셔보지 않는 수마트라 고양이
똥 커피에 대해 얘기하고 있던 중이었다. 찌푸린 채 입
으로만 웃는 나를 재이가 근심스런 표정으로 쳐다보았
다. 등에 차고 진득한 땀이 배어났다. 통증은 오래 가진
않았다. 섹스를 할 기분이 아니었지만 커피를 마시고
나서 재이의 목에 입을 맞추었다. 식사와 커피, 섹스는
정형화된 스케줄이었다. 다행히 재이는 중년 남성의 숨
겨진 사망 원인 중 복상사가 의외로 많다며 냉정하게 내
손을 밀어냈다. 오늘은 안 돼. 그런 깜찍함과 냉정함이
좋다. 물론 재이는 절대 제 집에서 재워주지도 않는다.
　통증은 사라졌는데 이마는 여전히 서늘한 느낌이다.

is. I had aloe cocktail and rose salad there for the first time too. It was fantastic."

"It didn't smell weird?"

"Nope."

Hearing him answer so firmly, Jae-i felt sorry that she had only brought out plain, ordinary coffee for him.

Different people see different sides of a person. One might notice his clear eyes; another, his long limbs, or his smile that brought wrinkles out near his eyes. Others might notice his money, power, or hidden cruel side. The first thing Jae-i noticed about him was his loneliness. The reason she couldn't say no to him when he held the elevator door open and asked her if she wanted to go see a movie was the obvious loneliness behinds his eyes. Since then, she'd seen many different sides of him, but whenever she thought of him the first thing she thought of was the loneliness she'd noticed in him the first time they'd met. Only, she didn't know that such gaudy intellectual vanity and life of a poseur would lie veiled behind his coffee dregs-colored loneliness.

He was drinking his coffee, when suddenly his eyebrows furrowed and he dropped his head.

뜨거운 물로 샤워를 하고 컴퓨터를 켰다. 아이들은, 아빠 잘 도착하셨어요? 라는 안부 이후로는 메일이 없다. 이만 돌아오라고 얘기하는 아빠가 두려운지도 모르겠다. 죽어도 돌아가지 않을 거야. 죽어도, 라는 말을 쓴 건 그 아이가 죽음을 모르기 때문이다. 메일 화면을 닫아버리고 이것저것 생각나는 단어를 검색칸에 쳐본다. ……마추픽추. LA에서 에어로 페루를 타고 가야 하는 잉카제국의 마지막 도시. 쿠스코에서 협궤열차를 타고 우르밤바 강 옆의 피삭에 도착하면 사라진 공중도시로의 여행이 시작된다. 태양에 바쳐진 영원한 제물처럼 산의 정상에 펼쳐진 놀라운 고대의 영화. 산사람의 가슴을 예리한 칼로 갈라 심장을 뜯어내서 제단에 바치는 제사. 그 제사의 희생 제물로 선택되는 것을 젊은이들은 지고의 영광으로 알았다. 뜨겁게 펄떡이는 젊은이의 심장을 뜯어내는 부분에서 재이는 약간 눈썹을 찌푸릴 것이며 언젠가는 마추픽추에 가보고 싶어, 중얼거릴 것이다. 쿠스코에 가면 한국인이 하는 라면가게가 있다는 얘기도 들려줘야지.

모든 검색어에 대해 컴퓨터는 더할 나위 없이 친절하고 자상하게 알려준다. 파리의 채식주의자 식당도, 샌

"What's wrong?"

His face, contorted as he seemed to stifle his pain, looked unfamiliar.

"If it hurts here, what's wrong?" He heaved out a long, thin breath. He placed his hand over his heart.

"How does it hurt?"

"It feels tight, or a bit stiff, and prickly."

"Since when?"

"It happened once before, two or three months ago."

"You should go get it checked. It could be your heart, or it could be acid reflux. That has similar symptoms."

"Huh. Which one's more critical?"

"The heart, of course."

"Then I'll go with that."

He began to laugh loudly, as if he had just told her a joke. Beads of sweat had formed lightly on his forehead.

*

A thin ray of light leaked through the entrance door. I must have left the light on before I left the

프란시스코 부둣가의 클램차우더 수프도, 파도가 미친 년처럼 머리채를 풀어헤치고 달려든다는 바닷가, 히피들의 천국이라는 코사무이 해변도 모두 인터넷이 알려준 것들이다. 출장을 자주 가긴 하지만 그런 곳까지 들를 여유는 없다. 시간도 돈도. 밤의 인터넷에는 외로운 인간들이 머리채를 풀어헤치고 달려든다. 혼자 지내는 밤마다 인터넷서핑을 하다보면 천일야화인들 재이에게 못 들려줄까.

재이에게 가면을 사주기로 했었지. 가면 카니발을 검색해본다. 베니스. 400여 개의 다리. 카사노바의 활동무대였던 불륜의 도시. 이 도시에는 유곽이 없다. 온 도시가 유곽이니까. 곤돌라 선착장 옆의 오래된 골목길로 들어서면 가면가게들이 있다. 진열장 아래 얌전히 누워 있는 가면들. 눈은 검게 열려 있고 입술은 닫혀 있어. 외로운 영혼을 부르는 표정으로 귀와 귀를 맞대고 나란히 누워 있지. 제 외로움의 주파수와 맞는 가면을 고르면 돼. 냉정하면서도 앙큼한 재이에겐 눈언저리가 황금분으로 치장된 창백한 석고가면이 어울릴 거야. 그 가면을 쓰고 길게 휘어진 황금 손톱을 손가락마다 붙이고 치렁한 망토를 걸친 채, 습기에 부식되어 가는 낡은 건

apartment in the morning. Out of the blue, the sound of my own voice rang in my ear. When the motion sensor light in my entranceway turns off automatically, even before I can turn the light on in my room. Did that show ever air? They'd told me the date and the time, but I couldn't remember. I didn't want to watch it anyway.

When I was having a cup of coffee at Jae-i's apartment, I felt an intense pain in my chest. It was an acute pain. It wasn't easy to suppress it and smile. I'd been talking about the Sumatran kopi lu-wak that I'd never had. Jae-i looked at me, worried, as I smiled with only my mouth while the rest of my face contorted in pain. A cold, sticky sweat had broken out on my back. The pain didn't last long. I didn't feel like having sex, but after I finished my coffee, I kissed Jae-i on her neck. Dinner, coffee, and sex. That was the usual schedule for us. Thankfully, Jae-i pushed my hand away, saying that one of the major undisclosed kinds of death for middle aged men was death by coition. *Not today*. I liked the cute, yet cool countenance she had. Of course, Jae-i wouldn't let me sleep over in her apartment either.

The pain had subsided, but my forehead still felt

물의 입구에 앉아 손톱을 펼친 채 키스를 한다면 모든 남루한 과거를 잊을 수 있을 거야. 재이. 이 이야기가 마음에 들어?

내게 어울리는 가면은 어떤 것일까. 가면을 하나씩 클릭해본다. 온통 검은, 뚫린 눈 부분이 오히려 희게 보이는 우울한 표정의 가면. 아니면.

아내는 내가 있는 동안 그래도 잘해주려 애를 썼다. 그런 아내가 연극배우처럼 느껴졌다. 팬들의 성원에 보답하기 위해 틈을 내서 지방공연을 내려온. 오래전에 식탁에 앉아 내뱉었던 자신의 말들, 나의 모든 것을 견딜 수 없다던 말들을 하나도 기억하지 못하는 듯한 그 표정. 일주일의 끝 날엔 무대막이 천천히 내려올 듯했던 하루하루. 오죽했으면 배 위에서 아내가 허리를 움직이고 있을 때 한군데도 닮지 않은 할리우드 여배우를 떠올려야 했을까. 사정하기 전에 나도 모르게 쓰다듬었던 아내의 등은 오전 열 시에 신문을 읽고 있을 때처럼 무표정하게 굳어 있었다.

금박이 화려한 이 가면은 아내에게도 어울릴 것이다. 하긴 썩은 물이 출렁거리는 베니스의 뒷골목, 어두운 건물 계단에 앉아 이 가면을 쓰고 두 번 휘어진 황금 손

cool. I took a hot shower and turned on the computer. Since their last email asking if I had a nice trip back to Korea, my children hadn't sent me another. Maybe they were scared of the dad who kept telling them to come home. I'm not going back even if it kills me. The reason she'd written "even if it kills" was she didn't know what death was. I closed the email window, and began to type any words that came into my mind into the search bar. Machu Picchu. The last city of the Inca Empire you can travel to from LA on Air Peru. When you take the narrow gauge train from Cuzco and arrive at Pisac near the Urubamba River, the journey to the vanished city in the sky begins. The remarkable glory of the ancient times stretched out on top of the mountain like an eternal sacrifice for the sun. A sacrifice that involved cutting open the chest of a living person and taking out the heart to offer it upon an altar. Inca youths believed that becoming a sacrifice was the highest honor they could attain. When I would tell her the part about ripping out the hot, throbbing heart out from a youth, Jae-i would frown slightly and murmur, I want to go to Machu Picchu some time. I'll also tell her that there's a Korean instant noodle restaurant in Cuzco.

톱을 달아준다면, 아내와 재이가 다를 게 무엇인가. 이 도시에서 살아가는 사람들에게 가면은 설탕보다, 화장지보다, 혹은 와인빛 루즈보다 더 필수품일 텐데.

*

"누구세요?"

"꽃배달 왔습니다."

그의 목소리다. 현관문을 여니 사람보다 먼저 장미꽃 다발이 코앞으로 쑥 다가온다.

식탁에 앉으며 그는 자신이 가져온 장미를 탐색하듯 지긋이 노려보았다.

"발칸의 장미야."

"발칸?"

"존재가 바로 고통인 땅이지. 아이러니컬하지 않아? 재이야. 미식가들이 수마트라 고양이똥 커피를 최고로 친다면 장미의 여왕은 단연 발칸의 장미야. 알바니아. 겨울엔 비와 진흙 때문에, 여름엔 먼지 때문에 숨을 쉴 수가 없는 곳이지만 그것보단 어디서 저격병의 총탄이 날아와 몸에 박힐지 모르는 처절한 내전의 땅이지. 그

The computer quite considerately provided me with all the information I needed or wanted. The vegetarian restaurant in Paris, clam chowder at the San Francisco wharf, the sea where the waves rush at you like a crazy woman with disheveled hair hanging loosely about her face, the beaches at Koh Samui, the paradise of hippies. These were all places that the internet had informed me of. I often went on business trips, but I had no time to stop by those places. Neither the time nor the money. Lonely people tear onto the internet at night with their hair disheveled. If I surfed the internet every night I spent alone, I'd be able to tell her all one thousand and one stories.

I told her I'd buy her a mask. I searched for mask carnivals. Venice. Over 400 bridges. The city of adultery. The city where Casanova lived. There was no red light district in that city because the whole city was a red light district. There were mask shops in the old alley next to the gondola dock. Masks quietly laid down in the display shelves. Their eyes hollow and their lips sealed. They look as if they are calling for lonely spirits. Laying side by side, their ears almost touching. You could just pick one that was on the same loneliness frequency level as

발칸 반도의 어둠이 흩어지기 전, 무거운 공기가 흔들리기 전, 자정부터 새벽 사이에 줄기를 자른, 강한 향기가 고스란히 가두어져 있는 그곳의 장미가 지상에서 가장 귀하게 대접받는 거야."

길거리 좌판에서 샀음이 분명한, 이미 끝이 검게 변색하기 시작한 장미 다발은 겉모습만은 비와 진흙으로 범벅된, 처절한 내전의 땅에서 온 것처럼 보였다. 종이 다발은 찢어져 있고 오늘이 지나면 쓰레기통으로 가야 할 꼴이다. 화병에서는 제대로 목도 가누지 못할 것 같아 재이는 현관에 있는 빈 못에 꽃다발을 거꾸로 걸어 두었다.

"드라이플라워로 만들어야겠어."

처음 사온 선물치곤 심했어, 라는 말을 삼키며 재이는 그렇게 말한다.

"장미는 여성의 은밀한 부위를 상징하지. 조지아 오키프의 장미 그림을 본 적이 있어? 그의 장미는 여성의 뜨거움과 파괴성과 습기와 매혹, 손대고 싶은 유혹을 성기보다 적나라하게 드러내고 있어. 너의 그것처럼."

목을 쓰다듬는 그의 눈빛이 은근해진다.

"나 오늘 나이트야."

you. Jae-I, you're cool but coy. A pale white plaster mask with gold shade around the eyes would be perfect for you. If you wear that mask, put the long, gold acrylic nails on your fingers, drape a long cape over your shoulders, and kiss me with your fingers outstretched as we sit on the front steps of an old building wearing away from the humidity. Then you'd be able to forget all your tired past. Jae-i, do you like this story?

Which mask would suit me? I clicked on each mask. A mask with a sad face, so black that it makes the hollow eyes slightly white. Or...

My wife tried to be good to me while I was there. But that made her feel even more like an actress. An actress on a regional tour to thank her fans for their support. She looked as if she couldn't remember anything she spat out at that table a long time ago—that she couldn't stand anything about me. Days passed. It felt as if a curtain would come down at the end of the week. It was horrible, to the point that I had to imagine a Hollywood actress who looked nothing like my wife as she moved her hips against my stomach. When my hands brushed her back in spite of myself, she felt stiff and ex-

"언제 나갈 거지?"

"지금."

"그래? 그럼 데려다줄게."

그는 금방 표정을 바꾼다. 끈적거리지 않는 그의 태도를 좋아하지만 이토록 쉽게 포기되는 열정도 서운하다. 핸드백을 들고 형광등 스위치를 내리기 전 잊었다는 듯 재이는 말한다.

"뒤에서 할래? 머리를 망가뜨리기 싫어서."

엉덩이 주사를 맞을 때처럼 이마를 약간 찌푸리며 재이는 스커트를 조심스럽게 걷어 올렸다. 오른손으로 재이의 팬티를 내리며 그는 왼손으로 스위치를 내린다. 여자가 가장 아름다울 땐 달빛 아래서야, 중얼거리며. 베란다 창으로 달이 보이진 않았지만 어둡지도 않다. 그가 몸을 움직이자 재이의 마음속에 희미했던 친밀감이 조금씩 커진다. 달은 없어, 속삭이자 손바닥으로 재이의 목덜미를 어루만진다. 달은, 네 눈 속에 있어. 공주의 엄지손톱만 한 작고 노란 달이 네 눈 속에. 깊은숨을 들이쉬는데 장미향이 비로소 느껴진다. 발칸의 장미? 그러고 보니 장미향 속에는 따스한 피에서 나는 비릿한 냄새가 섞여 있는 것 같기도 하다.

pressionless, just like my face reading a newspaper at ten in the morning.

This elaborately gilded mask would look nice on my wife. Well, if she put on this mask and curly golden nails, and sat on the steps of a dark building in a back alley in Venice where dirty water sloshed into the waterways, she wouldn't be all that different from Jae-i. For the people living in that city, masks were probably more of a necessity than sugar, toilet paper, or wine-colored lipstick.

*

"Who is it?"

"Flower delivery."

It was his voice. When she opened the door, a bouquet of roses greeted her before he did.

He sat down and passed his eyes over the roses he brought as if he was examining them.

"These are Balkan roses."

"Balkan?"

"Their existence is a suffering in and of itself. Isn't it ironic, Jae-i? If the coffee connoisseur says that the best coffee is Sumatran kopi luwak, then the queen of roses would definitely be the Balkan rose.

여름이 지나가고 있는지 아니면 채 식지 않은 몸의 열기 때문인지 바깥으로 나오자 뺨에 닿는 바람이 서늘하다. 신도시의 외곽에 있는 병원에 다다랐을 땐 가녀린 비가 뿌리기 시작했다.

"소독약 냄새보단 페인트 냄새가 더 강하게 날 것 같아."

"지은 지 얼마 되지 않았어. 내부는 호텔 수준이야."

"파리 캉봉 거리에 가면 샤넬이 죽을 때까지 살았던 리츠호텔이 있어. 다이애나 왕비가 죽기 전 연인과 마지막 만찬을 즐겼던 곳이지. 헤밍웨이는 그랬어. 천국의 꿈을 꿀 수 있다면 그곳은 리츠호텔이라고. 하지만 아무리 리츠호텔의 스위트룸 같아도 난 병원에선 한시도 머물고 싶지 않아. 재이야."

"간단해. 아프지 않으면 돼."

"넌 별걸 다 아는구나."

재이의 코끝을 그는 아프지 않게 살짝 눌러준다.

"나른하지?"

"나른하긴. 기운이 넘쳐."

재이는 남자의 눈동자를 들여다본다. 조금 전에 제 속의 정액을 다 쏟아 부은 여자에게까지도 끝내 지친 표

Albania. It's a place where you can't breathe because of the rain and the mud in the winter and because of the dust in the summer. But more than that, it's a miserable land overwrought with civil wars. You never know when a bullet from an enemy sniper will hit you. The roses are only cut from midnight until dawn, before the darkness subsides on the Balkan Peninsula, before the heavy air is shaken, the only time when the roses retain their powerful aroma. Those are the roses considered the rarest on this earth."

From the outside, the roses—surely bought on the street side, the edges of the petals already turning black—looked as if they really were from a miserable land overwrought with civil war, rain, and mud. The paper wrapping had been torn, and the roses look like they needed to be thrown out after today. If she put them in a vase, the roses would droop, so Jae-i hung them upside down on a nail near the front door.

"I'm going to dry them," Jae-i said, swallowing what she was thinking: this was ridiculous for a first present.

"A rose symbolizes a woman's private parts. Have you ever seen Georgia O'Keefe's paintings of ros-

정은 보이지 않는 남자. 생의 마지막 순간에도 포즈를 의식할 것 같은 남자. 늦었다. 돌아서 달려가는데 차창을 내리고 그가 외친다.

"잊지 마. 케타민. 귀찮게 구는 환자들에게 사흘만 주사해줘. 전부 퇴원해버릴 거야. 악몽보단 육체의 통증을 선택하는 게 인간이야."

*

오래전에 읽은 책을 펼쳐보면 붉은 색연필이나 심이 두터운 연필로 밑줄을 그은 문장을 만날 때가 있다. 어떤 건 다시 읽어보아도 왜 밑줄을 그었을까 이해할 수 없는 그런 문장도 있다. 사람도 그러하다. 이전에 좋아했던 사람을 다시 우연히 만나게 되었을 때 내가 이 사람의 어떤 면을 좋아했던 걸까, 도무지 알 수 없는 그런 일도 있다. 아내도 아마 그랬을 것이다. 한때는 내가 운명처럼 느껴진 순간도 있었을 것이다. 그러다가 언젠가부터 막이 내리기만을 기다리는 지친 배우처럼 우울한 얼굴 위에 웃음 띤 가면을 쓰고 견디기 시작했을 것이다. 더 이상 견딜 수 없어, 말하기 전까지. 우리 둘의 관

es? Her roses openly reveal the hotness, destruction, moisture, charm, and the temptation to touch even more than a woman's actual genitals. Just like yours."

His eyes flitted away as he stroked her neck.

"I have a night shift today."

"When are you heading out?"

"Now."

"Yeah? I'll take you." His face changed immediately. She liked that he wasn't clingy, but felt a bit hurt that he had given up so easily.

"Want to do it from behind?" Jae-i asked, holding her purse before turning off the light, as if she'd already forgotten what she'd said earlier. "I don't want to ruin my hair."

Jae-i carefully lifted her skirt up, frowning slightly as if she were about to receive a shot. As he slipped off her panties with his right hand, he turned off the light switch with his left. *A woman looks the most beautiful under the moonlight,* he murmured. She couldn't see the moon through the balcony window, but it wasn't dark either. As he started to move, a faint sense of intimacy began to grow in Jae-i's heart. *There is no moon,* Jae-i whispered, and he stroked the back of her neck. *The*

계의 끝 어디쯤 두터운 무대막이 내려올 것을 예감하고 있긴 했지만 이토록 상투적인 반전까지 준비되어 있을 줄은 몰랐다. 아내는 묻고 있었다. 메일 속에서.

……무얼 위해서 이 상태를 더 견뎌야만 하는가, 하는 생각이 들어. 더 이상 뭐가 두려운 거지? 짐작하고 있겠지만 이런 상황을 정리하고 그 사람과 새로 시작하고 싶어. 당신에게 원하는 건 아무것도 없어. 나로선 헤어져 지내는 동안 뭔가 긍정적인 변화가 있길 바랐는데 지난번 당신이 여기 왔을 때, 당신의 얼굴을 봤을 때 깨달았어. 바뀔 수 있는 건 남아 있지 않다고.

*

초인종 소리를 듣고 나온 재이는 현관문 밖에 서 있는 사람이 그라는 걸 알고는 얼굴을 살짝 찌푸린다. 약속 없이 제멋대로 드나드는 건 싫다. 현관 앞에서 돌려보내려 했는데 문 앞에 서 있는 그의 얼굴을 보고는 현관문을 조금 더 열어주었다. 감추기엔 너무 커다란 돌이 가슴에 얹혀 있는 눈빛이다.

"무슨 일이에요?"

moon is in your eyes. A tiny yellow moon, the size of
Thumbelina's thumbnail, is in your eyes. When she
took a deep breath, she was able to smell the roses at last. Balkan roses? Come to think of it, there
seemed to be a slight hint of fish and fresh blood
mixed with the fragrance of the roses.

Because the summer was almost over, or maybe
because her body had not yet cooled down, the
wind on her cheek felt cool and lovely outside.
When they arrived at the hospital on the outskirts
of the city, a misty rain began to fall.

"It looks like it'll smell more like paint than anes-
thetics," he commented.

"It was only built recently. Inside, though, it looks
like a nice hotel."

"On Rue Cambon in Paris, there's the Ritz Hotel
where Chanel lived until she died. It was also
where Princess Diana had her last meal with her
lover. And Hemingway once said, you can dream
of paradise at the Ritz Hotel. But, even if it looks
like a suite at the Ritz Hotel, I don't want to stay at
the hospital even for a second, Jae-i."

"Well then, it's simple. Don't get sick."

"You know everything, huh."

He squished the tip of her nose with his finger.

"커피가 마시고 싶어서."

"난 수마트라고양이가 아닌데."

"그러고 보니 재이는 고양이를 닮았어."

그뿐 그의 수다는 더 이상 이어지지 않았다. 커피를 갈고 여과지에 담아 스위치를 누르고 다시 식탁에 앉을 때까지도 그는 조용하다. 이건 익숙하지가 않아. 재이는 그가 입고 있는 셔츠를 화제에 올려본다.

"버버리 셔츠네. 늘 명품만 입어."

"집사람이 보내줬어."

재이는 그의 얼굴을 쳐다보았다. 무슨 얘기가 하고 싶은 것일까, 오늘. 내 앞에서 한 번도 아내 얘기를 한 적이 없는데.

"아내는, 미국에 있어."

처음 듣는 것처럼 물었다.

"그래요? 떨어져 살아보니 어때?"

"집사람은 내 열렬한 팬이야. 아침저녁으로 메일을 보내지. 계절이 바뀔 땐 이렇게 옷도 보내고."

그가 원하는 건 나의 질투심일까. 커피를 가지러 일어나며 재이는 그의 셔츠 뒤쪽을 뒤집어보았다. 셔츠는 이미테이션이다. 재이는 모른 척한다.

"Tired?"

"Not at all. I'm all awake."

Jae-i stared into his eyes. The man who never shows a look of exhaustion, even to the woman in whom he poured all of himself just moments ago. The man who seemed like he would make sure to keep his cool even in the last moments of his life.

She was late. She turned around and rushed to the hospital as he pulled down the window and shouted, "Don't forget! Ketamine! Give it to annoying patients for three days! They'll all leave. It's only human to choose physical pain over nightmares!"

*

When I look through books I've read a long time ago, sometimes there are sentences underlined with red color pencil or a pencil with a thick lead. Some sentences, I don't know why I underlined them even when I read them again. People are like that too. When I run into people I used to like, sometimes I wonder, what did I actually liked about this person before? I can never figure it out. My wife probably felt that way too. At one point, she might have thought we were made for each other.

"그래, 이런 건 선물이 아니면 선뜻 사긴 어려워. 예쁘네. 자긴 어때?"

"뭐가?"

"당신 와이프."

"좋지도, 나쁘지도 않아."

그 말은 아내에 대한 얘기가 아니라 방금 한 모금 마신 커피에 대한 품평처럼 들린다. 익숙하지 않은 침묵을 지키며 앉아 있던 그는 커피잔을 내려놓고 성급하게 재이를 껴안는다. 뭔진 모르지만 오늘은 다 받아주마, 하는 기분으로 재이는 바지의 지퍼를 내렸다. 몸속으로 들어오기 전, 그는 재이의 눈을 들여다보며 진지하게 묻는다.

"너, 나 사랑하니?"

이런 질문은 정말 싫다는 걸 왜 모를까. 자기답지 않게. 재이는 대답 대신 그의 목을 끌어안는다. 그는 다만 섹스가 하고 싶어 찾아온 사람처럼 손이 미끄러지도록 땀을 흘리며 재이의 몸 안으로 파고들었다. 사랑을 나눈다기보다 불안하게 쫓기는 사람 같다.

"나, 차가운 물 좀 가져다줄래요?"

죽은 사람처럼 엎드린 그가 너무 무거워 물을 가져다

But then, from some point of time and on, she began to only endure everything about me, wearing a smiling mask on her sad face like a tired actress waiting for the curtain to fall. Until she said, I can't stand it anymore.

I knew that one day, somewhere near the end of our relationship, a heavy curtain would fall, but I had no idea that there'd be such a conventional plot twist waiting for me. My wife was saying to me in an email:

I keep wondering, what it is that we have to keep on maintaining? What am I afraid of at this point? I'm sure you've probably assumed already, but I want to start my life over with him. I don't want anything from you. I was hoping that things would change for the better while we stayed apart, but the last time when you came, when I saw your face, I knew. There's nothing that can change anymore.

*

When the bell rang, Jae-i walked out of her room to get the door. But then seeing that it was him standing outside, she frowned slightly. She didn't

달라고 말할 때까지 그는 재이의 가슴 위에 젖은 빨래처럼 엎드려 있었다. 재이는 냉장고로 걸어가는 그의 벗은 뒷모습을 바라보았다. 큰 키에 비해 어깨도 좁고 엉덩이도 무척 작다. 연민을 느끼고 싶지 않아 재이는 베개에 얼굴을 묻는다. 재이가 물을 다 마시기를 기다려 그는 조심스럽게 묻는다.

"자고 가도 돼?"

재이는 코를 살짝 찌푸리며 고개를 젓는다.

*

어둠 속을 더듬더듬 걸어가다 책상 모서리에 부딪친다. 모니터가 환하게 밝아온다. 나는 몰래 도망가다 들킨 아이처럼 의자에 털썩 주저앉았다. 재이의 집에서 자고 싶었던 건 아니다. 집으로 돌아와 아내의 질문에 대답할 일이 두려웠을 뿐이다. 뭐가 두려운 거지? 혼자 남는 것? 언제부터 혼자였는데. 아이들과의 이별? 죽어도, 죽어도 돌아가고 싶지 않아. 그때부터 이별이었다. 나는, 그저 너무나 넓은 바깥에 쫓겨나 있을 뿐이다. 아내와 아이들이 살고 있는, 튀김 기름과 찌개 냄새가 밴

like it when he arrived at her doorstep at will, as if it didn't matter when he came calling. She was going to turn him away at the door, but when she saw his face she opened the door a little wider. His eyes seemed to say that there was a huge stone, too big to hide, on his chest.

"What is it?"

"I just wanted some coffee."

"I'm not a Sumatran civet."

"Come to think of it, you do look like a cat."

That was it. He said little after that. She ground the coffee beans, poured the powder into the filter, pressed the switch, and sat back at the table. The whole time, he was quiet. It was strange. She decided to talk about his shirt.

"Burberry. You always wear expensive brands."

"My wife sent it to me."

Jae-i looked at him. What was it that he wanted to say today? He had never mentioned his wife in front of her.

"My wife... She's in the US."

"Really? How does it feel, living apart?" Jae-i asked as if she was finding this out for the first time.

"My wife is a huge fan of me. She sends me

그 작고 환한 아파트의 바깥, 이토록 넓은 바깥에.

자꾸 목이 마르다. 차가운 물을 한 잔 들고 부엌 유리창에 비친 내 얼굴을 바라보며 웃어 보았다. 누군가에겐 견딜 수 없는 웃음. 손가락으로 오른쪽 눈썹 위쪽의 머리카락을 왼쪽으로 넘겨보았다. 가르마는 바꿀 수 있을지도 모르겠다. 손을 떼자 머리는 원래 자리로 돌아온다. 손바닥에 스치는 이마가 싸늘하다.

다시 통증이 밀려온다. 커피 때문일 것이다. 혹은 커피를 마신 후의 격한 섹스 때문일 것이다. 누군가가 강철기구로 가슴을 조이는 듯하다. 보이지 않는 그 기구를 뜯어내기라도 하듯 나는 손을 등 뒤로 휘저어본다. 아무것도 잡히지 않는다. 그러지 마, 제발. 의자에서 일어서려 했다. 마음은 일어서는데 몸은 책상에 엎드린다. 몸은 작게 오그리고 싶은 듯하다. 비명조차 지를 수없다. 머릿속이 점액질의 액체처럼 불규칙하게 출렁거린다. 고통은 짧은 순간에 극심해진다. 견딜 수 없어, 당신의 모든 것을. 웃는 모습도, 가르마도. 마이클과 에밀리. 죽어도, 죽어도 돌아가고 싶지 않아. 내게만 쓰라렸던 피셔먼스워프의 햇살. 안방등을 켜기 전에 현관등이 꺼졌을 때 나를 덮쳐오던 어두움. ……이상하구나. 어

emails day and night. She sends me clothes too when the seasons change."

Does he want me to be jealous? She stood up to get the coffee and quickly flipped the collar of his shirt. It was a fake. Jae-i pretended not to have noticed.

"Well, it's hard to buy shirts like that unless for a present. It looks nice. What do you think?"

"About what?"

"Your wife."

"Not great, but not bad."

It sounded as if he was talking about the coffee he had just drunk, not his wife. He sat there in an unfamiliar state of silence, and then he put down his coffee mug, and hurriedly embraced Jae-i. Jae-i didn't know what this was all about, but she decided to just take it for today and unzipped her pants.

"Do you love me?" he asked her with a deep, somber look on his face. He looked her in the eyes before he came inside of her.

How does he not know that I hate questions like that? That's not like him.

Instead of giving him an answer, she hugged him tightly. As if he came to see her just for sex, he

쩌면 이토록 짧은 순간에, 이토록 많은 기억들이 밀려올 수 있는 걸까. 파도가 미친년처럼 머리를 풀고 달려드는 코사무이 해변의 격랑처럼. 모든 파도가 일순에 덮쳐오듯 비일상적으로, 현실감 없이.

그렇게 모든 기억들이, 그리고 알 수 없는 것들에 대한 후회가 밀려오는군.

어쩔 수 없이.

*

위쪽을 향해 일제히 등을 돌린 사람들이 재이의 집 앞까지 막고 서 있었다. 재이는 키를 꽂으며 위쪽을 올려다보았다. 사람들이 안쪽을 들여다보지 못하게 막고 있던 경관이 재이를 쳐다보더니 안에 대고 뭐라고 얘기를 한다. 숱이 적은 머리에 재이보다도 키가 작은 남자 하나가 나와 손짓을 한다. 계단에 서 있던 사람들이 갈라지며 길을 내주었다.

"아래층에 사십니까?"

"그런데요."

"며칠 사이 위층에서 무슨 이상한 기척을 못 느꼈어

burrowed into her, sweating to the point that his hands began to slip. He didn't seem like he was making love. It seemed like he was being pursued.

"Can you get me a glass of cold water?"

He lay still on her bosom like wet laundry until Jae-i asked him to get her a glass of water, unable to stand his corpse-like weight anymore. She watched his naked body from the back as he walked toward the refrigerator. He was tall, but his shoulders were narrow, and his rear, small for his height. She didn't want to feel sympathy for him, and so Jae-i buried her face in the pillow. He waited for Jae-i to finish drinking before he spoke.

"Can I sleep here tonight?" he asked carefully.

Wrinkling her nose slightly, Jae-i shook her head.

*

I fumbled my way in the darkness, but ended up bumping into the corner of the desk. The computer monitor blinked on. I dropped into the chair like a child caught attempting to secretly run away. It wasn't that I wanted to sleep at Jae-i's apartment. I was afraid of coming home and responding to my wife's email. What was I afraid of? Being alone? I'd

요? 비명소리나 다투는 소리 같은."

"무슨 일인데요?"

"혼자 살고 있었던 것 같은데. 마루에 쓰러져 있었습니다. 연락 없이 출근하지 않아 회사에서 나와 본 모양이에요."

마루에 놓인 들것에 그는 눕혀져 있다. 자고 가도 돼? 그날 밤 입었던 버버리 셔츠를 입은 팔이 흰 시트 틈으로 보인다. 재이는 고개를 저었다.

"전혀 모르겠어요."

사실은 아무것도 궁금해하지 않는 듯한 표정의 그 경관과, 몇 가지 질문과 대답을 주고받는 동안 재이는 오래전에 보았던 영화의 장면이 생각났다. 젊은 날의 말론 브란도가 나왔던. 까맣게 잊고 있었던 영화의 장면이 어쩜 이렇게 생생하게 기억날까. 난 몰라요. 그 남자를 몰라요. 고개를 젓던 여자의 깜찍한 표정. 삶과 영화는 어느 순간부터 서로를 표절하는 것 같다.

모른다는 게 터무니없는 거짓말은 아니다. 재이는 함께 지내지 않을 때의 그에 대해선 거의 몰랐다. 마지막 입었던 셔츠가 그를 무척 사랑하는 아내가 보내준 선물이라는 것, 그리고 그 셔츠가 유사상표일 뿐이라는 것,

been alone for a while. Being separated from my kids? *I don't want to go back even if it kills me. Even if it kills me.* We'd been separated from then. I've just been kicked out to the vast outside world. To this vast outside world, outside that small, bright apartment, which smelled of frying oil and stew, where my wife and children were.

I kept getting thirsty. I held a glass of cold water and smiled at my reflection in the kitchen window. A smile someone couldn't stand. I brushed the hair over my right eyebrow to the left. I might be able to change the part in my hair. When I took my hand off my hair, it all came back to where it had been. My forehead felt cold in my hand.

The pain was lapping up inside of me again. It was probably because of the coffee. Or the sex after the coffee. It felt as if someone was kneading my heart with an iron clamp from the back. As if I were trying to release that invisible clamp, I flung my arms to the back. But I was only grabbing at the air. *Stop. Please.* I tried to stand up from the chair. I stood up in my mind, but my body toppled onto the desk. My body seemed to want to curl up into a small ball. I couldn't even scream. The insides of my head were spilling all over the walls of

정도 외에는. 그는 셔츠가 오리지널이 아니라는 사실을 몰랐을까. 그런데 그날, 그 셔츠가 진짜가 아니라는 걸 자신은 왜 말해주지 않았을까. 말한다면 그가 재이에게 퍼부었던 길고도 현란했던 진술들이 대부분 진실이 아님을 알고 있는 것처럼 보일까봐 그랬던 건 아닐까. 남루한 삶을 이어가기 위해서는 생각보다 많은 비밀이 필요하지.

현관문을 열고 들어오자 마른 장미 다발이 보인다. 인생의 알싸한 향기도 어둠과 고통 속에서 축적되는 것일진대 향기로 응축되기엔 너무 독한 어떤 것이 그의 생에 있었을까.

현관등이 어느 순간 꺼져버린다. 어둠 속에 가만히 서있자 뭔가 가슴 밑바닥에서 희미하게 출렁거리기 시작한다. 잘 몰랐었는데, 그가 있음으로 해서 생의 순간이 풍요로웠던 적도 있었다는 생각이 든다. 현관등이 꺼지고 안방등이 켜지기 전, 어둠 속에서 그의 마음도 이렇게 조금 추웠을까. 천일야화의 세헤라자데는 긴 이야기 끝에 목숨을 건졌는데 그의 적은 술탄보다 더 냉혹한 것이었는지. 그가 했던 무수한 말들을 허탄한 웃음 끝에 잊어버리곤 했지만 그가 없는 지금, 그것들이 꼭 거

my skull like jelly. The pain was tremendous within moments. *I can't stand it, everything about you. The way you smile, the part in your hair.* Michael and Emily. *I don't want to go back even if it kills me. Even if it kills me.* The sunlight stinging on my skin. The darkness that swoops over me when the motion sensor light in the entranceway turns off automatically, even before I can turn the light on in my room. Strange. How can so many memories rush at you in such a short period of time? Just like the raging waves at the beach in Koh Samui that rush at you like a crazy woman with disheveled hair. As if all the waves were rushing at you, all at once. Unusually. Surreal.

All those memories, and regrets about things I didn't know were rushing at me.

Inevitably.

*

People were standing around, staring upward and blocking even her apartment. As she slipped the key into the lock Jae-i looked toward where the people were. A police officer blocking people from looking in noticed Jae-i and said something to someone inside. A balding man, shorter than Jae-i,

짓은 아니었다는 생각이 들기도 한다.

하긴 알바니아에서 가져와야만 발칸의 장미일까. 짙은 안개가 낀 날이면 안개에 몸을 가리고 눈물도 감추고 노래하며 춤을 추다 저격병의 총탄에 피를 흘리며 쓰러지는 것, 웃고 있는 등 뒤로 누군가가 총을 겨누고 있는 것, 소멸의 시점을 알 수 없는 것, 먼지와 안개와 진흙과 결핍을 익숙하게 받아들여야만 하는 것, 그건 그곳이나 여기나 마찬가지일 것이다.

재이는 마른 장미 다발을 못에서 내려 쓰레기통에 넣었다. 여름의 끝이라 해도 아직 더웠다. 미약한 부패의 냄새가 번지고 있었다. 날카롭고 차가운 느낌이 머릿속을 꿰뚫고 지나간다. 자고 가도 돼? 그날 밤이었을 것이다. 저격용 베레타를 들고 있지 않은 제 손을 재이는 물끄러미 내려다보았다. 그가 쓰러지기 전까지 무수하게 박혔던 보이지 않는 총탄 중 하나가 이 손에서 날아간 건 아니었을까.

재이는 처음 그와 영화를 보았던 날 샀던 시디를 찾아 플레이어에 올려놓았다. 영화를 보는 중간에 살짝 졸았는데 그는 알고 있었을까. 그 영화는 정말이지 재미가 없었다. 기억나는 건 밤의 주차장을 빠져나가는 두

walked out and gestured at her. The people who had been standing in the stairwell parted to make way for him.

"Do you live here?"

"Yes."

"Have you heard anything strange upstairs recently? Screaming or arguing?"

"What's going on?"

"He must have been living alone. He was lying on the floor. He didn't come in to work, so they sent someone to check on him."

He was lying on a stretcher on the floor. *Can I sleep here tonight?* Through the white sheets, she could see his arm, clothed in the Burberry shirt he had worn that night.

"I don't know," Jae-i shook her head.

She answered few of the police officer's questions. The officer seemed like he wasn't curious at all, and Jae-i recalled a scene from a movie she'd seen a long time ago. The one with a young Marlon Brando. How was it possible that the scene she'd completely forgotten about now came to mind so vividly all of a sudden? I don't know. I don't know him. The woman in the film had looked completely innocent as she shook her head. It seemed that life

살인자의 모습뿐. 졸음에 겨워 눈을 반쯤 뜬 채로, 텅 빈 밤의 주차장이 뜻밖에 아름답다는 생각을 했을 뿐이다.

질문을 할 수 없는 곳으로 가버린 후에야 그의 수다스러웠던 생의 이면이 약간은 궁금해진다. 가사를 들려주던 그의 목소리도 조금은 그리워진다. 그가 몸속으로 들어와 천천히 움직이기 시작할 때면 생겨나던 희미한 친밀감이 뜬금없이 사물거린다. 재이는, 어쩐지 밤마다 그가 들려주던 이야기의 끝을 알고 있었던 것 같기도 하다. 잊은 줄 알았는데 노래의 가사가 선명하게 떠오른다.

여름의 끝이 이토록 아름다웠던 적은 없었네.
헤어지기에 이토록 아름다운 순간은 없었네.

『발칸의 장미를 내게 주었네』, 아시아, 2014

and film begin to plagiarize each other at a certain point.

It wasn't a complete lie to say that she didn't know him. She didn't know anything about him when he was not with her. The last shirt he had ever worn was the one his loving wife had sent him as a gift. The shirt had been a fake. That was about all she knew. Had he known that the shirt wasn't an original? Why hadn't she told him that the shirt wasn't an original that day? Maybe because she'd been afraid that if she had, he might have found out that she knew all those long, elaborate stories he told her were mostly false. You need to keep a lot more secrets than you think to continue your tired, old life.

As soon as she opened the door and walked into the living room, she noticed the dry bouquet of roses. The piquant scent of life accrued in darkness and pain. Had there been something so strong, so poisonous that you just couldn't be condensed into one scent?

The motion sensor light in the entranceway went out automatically. She stood still in the darkness and felt something spilling out from the bottom of her heart. She hadn't realized it before, but it suddenly struck her that at times her life had been full because of him. In that darkness, after the motion sensor light in the entranceway went off automatically, but before he turned on the light in his room, had he also felt a slight chill in his heart? Scheherazade of the *One Thousand and One Nights* was able to escape death after narrating her thousand stories. Maybe his enemy was even crueler than the sultan. She used to forget the many things he told her with a hollow laugh, but now, with him gone, she thought that they might not have all been lies.

Well, a rose doesn't need to come from Albania to be a Balkan rose. Holding your tears back, singing, and dancing in a heavy fog, and then falling down, blood pouring out of you from an enemy bullet. Someone standing and pointing a rifle at the back of a laughing man. Not knowing the time of your death. Having to accept dust, fog, mud, and loss with an old sense of familiarity. All of that were probably the same here as well.

Jae-i took the bouquet of dry roses down and threw them into the trashcan. Although summer was coming to an end, it was still hot. There was already a faint smell of decay. Something cold and sharp pierced her head. *Can I sleep over tonight?* It was probably that night. Jae-i looked down at her hands. There was no Beretta sniper there. Could one of the invisible bullets that bore into him until he collapsed have left these hands?

Jae-i inserted the CD he'd bought for her on the day she'd gone to see a movie with him into the CD player. She'd dozed off in the middle of the film. Had he known? The movie had been incredibly monotonous. The only scene she remembered from the film was the two murderers leaving the parking lot at night. With her eyes half open from sleep, she had thought that the empty parking lot at night was unexpectedly beautiful.

Only after he had gone to a place where she couldn't ask him questions, she now became a bit curious about his garrulous world. She began to miss his voice, reciting the lyrics to the French song. A little bit. The faint trace of intimacy that slowly arose in her when he came inside of her. It stirred and shifted inside her all of a sudden. Jae-i thought that she maybe knew the end of the stories he told her every night. The lyrics to the song she thought she'd forgotten came to her in full, clear detail.

The end of summer had never been so beautiful.
And no moment was more beautiful for us to part.

Translated by Stella Kim

해설

Afterword

아플수록 향기로워지는

정실비 (문학평론가)

어떤 사람은 아무 생각 없이 말하기도 하지만, 어떤 사람은 죽지 않기 위해 말한다. 퍼셔먼스 워프의 클램 차우더 수프에 대해, 몽마르트 언덕의 홍합요리와 방콕 야시장의 볶음국수에 대해, 끊임없이 말하는 남자가 있다면 어느 쪽일까. 이 이국적인 울림의 단어들이 모두 애써 만들어낸 거짓말의 일부라면, 이 남자는 죽지 않기 위해 말하는 사람일 것이다. 정미경 소설의 주인공인 이 남자의 삶은 거짓된 말과 거짓된 표정으로 빼곡히 채워져 있다.

독자는 소설을 읽으며 남자의 이야기에서 사실인 것과 거짓인 것을 추려내 차가운 대차대조표를 작성해볼

The More Painful, The More Fragrant

Jeong Sil-bi (literary critic)

Some people talk without thinking, but other people talk to survive. If there is a man who incessantly talks about clam chowder at Fisherman's Wharf, steamed mussels on Monmartre, and stir-fried noodles at the Bankok night market, would he be the former or the latter? If these words with an exotic ring to them are all lies he laboriously concocted, then he probably is one of those people who talk to survive. This man is the protagonist of a short story, written by Jung Mi-kyung. His life is packed full of lies and deceitful facial expressions. While reading the story, the readers can probably make a list of lies and truths from everything he

수도 있을 것이다. 예컨대 남자는 재이에게 출장에 다녀왔다고 말했지만 사실은 가족을 만나기 위한 여행을 다녀온 것이고, 재이에게 언젠가 클램차우더 수프를 사주겠다고 말할 것이지만 그럴 일은 없을 것이라는 것 등등. 그러나 이러한 독법은 이 소설을 읽는 좋은 방법이 아닌 것 같다. 이 소설에서 중요한 것은 이야기의 진위 여부가 아니라 이야기의 지속 여부이기 때문이다. 정미경은 그래서 남자를 세헤라자데에 비유한다. 죽지 않기 위해 매일 밤 왕에게 이야기를 들려줬던 세헤라자데처럼, 남자는 외로움이라는 감정에 짓눌려 죽지 않기 위해 재이에게 쉴 새 없이 이야기한다.

남자의 이야기에 늘 얼마간 거짓이 섞여 있다는 것을 재이는 알고 있다. 그러나 재이는 분노하거나 슬퍼하지 않는다. 그들은 "서로의 은닉된 삶의 한 조각씩을 이토록 풍요롭게, 이토록 인색하게 보여주는 것 이상은 원하는 게 없"다. 오히려 이 소설에서 '진실'은 섣불리 발설되어서는 안 되는 것이며 쉽사리 발견되어서도 안 되는 비밀스러운 것이다. 어떤 진실은 너무도 잔인하고 가혹하여 그것을 말하는 자와 듣는 자의 관계를 회복불능의 상태로 만들어버리기 때문이다. 남자의 아내가 어느 날

says. For instance, the man tells Jae-i that he went on a business trip, but he had actually been to see his family; he tells her that he will one day treat her clam chowder, but that won't happen, and so on. However, this is not a good way to read this story. Whether his stories are true or not is not the focus of this short story. The important thing is whether the stories will continue or not. Jung likens him to Scheherazade. Just like Scheherazade who told the king stories to save herself, the man continuously tells Jae-i stories to keep himself from suffocating under the weight of loneliness.

Jae-i knows that all of his stories contain lies to a certain extent. But Jae-i is not infuriated or sad about it. They "share small parts of their veiled lives in abundant, yet sparing manner. [And there] is nothing they want more." In fact, "truth" is a secret in this story; it is something that must not be carelessly blurted out or discovered easily. Some truths are too cruel and brutal. They can ruin the relationship between the speaker and the listener to a point of no return, just like the way the relationship between the man and his wife was destroyed the moment the man's wife said, "I can't stand you anymore. Everything. The way you eat your soup, the

돌연 "당신을 견딜 수 없어. 모든 걸. 국을 떠먹는 모습도, 수그린 머리의 가르마도, 웃는 모습도, 엎드려서 신문을 들여다보는 것도, 그 모든 게."라고 말하는 순간, 두 사람의 관계가 파탄 나듯이.

아내가 사라진 자리에 들어서는 것은 거대한 외로움의 덩어리다. 이 감정의 부피는 너무 커서 남자가 애써 가리려 해도 그를 처음 보는 사람의 눈에도 포착될 정도다. 그래서 재이가 그를 생각할 때 제일 먼저 떠올리는 것은 그를 "처음 보았던 순간의 외로움"이다. 외로움에 관한 소설은 많다. 그러나 도시에 사는 중산층 이상의 사람들의 외로움에 관해서라면 정미경만큼 섬세하게 내면을 어루만지는 작가도 드물 것이다. 정미경은 외로움이라는 감정이 한 인간의 내면에서 어떻게 움직이고 자라나는지 구체적으로 그려낸다. 예컨대 "현관등이 꺼지고 안방등이 켜지기 전"의 시간 동안 엄습하는 외로움에 대한 묘사를 보라. 물리적으로는 찰나의 시간이지만 심리적으로는 영겁의 시간이기도 한 시간을 정미경은 현학적인 어휘나 장황한 미사여구 대신 일상의 사물을 통해 담백하게 표현해낸다.

그리하여 정미경은 환하고 작은 집에서 쫓겨나와 덩

part in your hair I see when you bend your head, the way you laugh, the way you sleep, the way you read your newspaper while lying on your belly... Everything." What fills the space his wife had once occupied is massive loneliness. This emotion is so massive that despite his desperate attempt to hide it, even a stranger notices it at first sight. That is the reason "the loneliness she saw in him at their first encounter" is the first thing Jae-i recalls when thinking about him. There are many novels and short stories about loneliness. However, in terms of the loneliness of middle class Koreans living in a city, writers like Jung who can gently and delicately embrace them are rare. Jung paints a detailed picture of loneliness moving and growing within oneself. Let's take a look at her description of loneliness that suddenly sneaks up on the man during the few seconds after the automatic light at the entrance turns off and before he turns on the light in his room. Even though physically it is only a few seconds, psychologically it can last an eternity. Instead of using pedantic terms or wordy and flowery expressions, she simply gets to the point using objects that we use in our daily lives.

In such a way, Jung silently molds and places in

그러니 바깥에 앉아 있는 남자, 아내가 싫어하는 가르마 정도는 바꿔볼 수 있지 않을까 하며 손가락으로 머리카락을 넘겨보는 남자, 그러나 결국 "어쩔 수 없이" 심장이 멈춰버리는 남자의 형상을 조용히 빚어 우리 앞에 내려놓는다. 가족 없이 죽어간 한 남자의 삶을 섬세하게 어루만지는 것, 이것은 정미경이 소설가로서 지닌 드물고도 따뜻한 능력이다. 남자의 삶을 향하여 위선적이라고 손가락질하는 것은 쉬운 일이지만 그러한 위선이 '불가피'하여 아이러니한 삶의 조건을 '이해'하는 일은 쉽지 않은 일이기 때문이다. 이 소설은 인간에 대한 도덕적 재단이 아닌 유연한 이해에서 출발하고 있으며, 그렇기 때문에 특수한 한 남자의 이야기로 읽히는 데에 그치지 않고 보편적인 인간의 숙명에 관한 이야기로 읽힌다. 그리하여 이 소설은 우리로 하여금 어느 사이엔가 "남루한 삶을 이어가기 위해서는 생각보다 많은 비밀이 필요"하다는 말에 고개를 끄덕이게 하고, 사실과 거짓 사이에서 위태롭게 서 있는 자신의 두 발을 바라보게 한다.

그러나 자신의 위치를 깨닫게 하는 것이 이 소설의 유일한 목적은 아닐 것이다. 정미경은 고개를 숙이고

front of us the shape of a man who has been kicked out of a small, brightly lit house and is sitting alone outside; a man who flips his hair with his finger, thinking he can change the part in his hair that his wife hates; but a man whose heart stops "inevitably." Gently embracing the life of a man who dies, separated from his family. This is a rare and "sincere" ability Jung has as a writer. It is easy to scorn the man's life, saying he is a hypocrite, but it is difficult to "understand" the ironic situation his life is in where such hypocrisy is "inevitable."

This story takes off from a supple understanding —not an ethical judgment—of human beings. As a result, this story does not stop at being a story about a peculiar man. It reads as a story about the universal fate of human beings. Therefore this story makes the readers nod their heads when she writes, "To continue living your shabby life, you need to keep a lot more secrets than you think you need," and look down at their own two feet, as they stand precariously between lies and truths.

"A Rose of the Balkans," however, not only makes the readers realize their positions in life. Jung presents a "rose of the Balkans" at our feet, as we stand with our heads bowed. A rose of the Balkans

서 있는 우리의 발치에 '발칸의 장미'를 바친다. 발칸의 장미는 비와 진흙과 먼지와 총탄을 견디며 처절한 내전의 땅에서 피어난 꽃이다. 방금 쓴 문장의 주어는 '인간'으로 바꾸어도 무방하다. 인간은 발칸의 장미처럼 비와 진흙과 먼지와 총탄을 견디며 피어날 것이고, 때로는 심장을 움켜쥐고 쓰러진 남자처럼 시들기도 할 테지만, 피어나고 시들며 남자와 재이처럼 어떠한 "생의 순간" 잠시나마 서로를 풍요롭게 만들어주기도 할 것이다. 정미경은 인간을 장미에 비유함으로써 진실이 두려워 짐짓 모른 체하고 있는 이에게, 그리고 진실에 압도당해 울고 있는 이에게, 독특한 위로를 건넨다. 당신의 생에 응축된 그 "어둠과 고통"으로 인해 당신은 향기롭다고. 어두워질수록, 고통스러워질수록, 향기 또한 진해질 것이라고. 이것이 정미경이 생을 끌어안는 방식이며, 이 소설이 생을 긍정하는 방식이다.

blooms in the miserable land of civil wars, enduring the rain, dirt, dust, and bullet showers. The
subject of the previous sentence can be changed
to human. Humans, like roses of the Balkans,
would bloom, enduring the rain, dirt, dust, and
bullets. We might wither, like the man who collapsed from a heart attack. But as they bloom and
wither, they would make others' lives full—even if it
is only a short period of time—in certain "moments
of [their lives]." By comparing humans to roses,
Jung consoles those who pretend to not know the
truth because they are afraid of it, and those who
are crying under the weight of the truth. She says
that the "darkness and the pain" condensed in our
lives make us fragrant. The darker and more pain-
ful our lives get, our fragrance will become more
powerful. This is the way Jung embraces life, and
the way this short story affirms life.

비평의 목소리

Critical Acclaim

서사구조의 고전적 안정감, 미묘한 정서를 옮겨 담는 섬세한 문체, 존재와 삶을 응시하는 강렬한 시선, 이 세 가닥의 튼실한 끈이 수놓은 풍경은 요즘의 우리 문단에서 찾아보기 어려운 새로운 에너지를 내뿜고 있다. 배수아보다는 고전적이며, 전경린보다 차분하고, 공지영보다 다양하면서, 신경숙보다 세련된, 그리고 은희경보다는 절실한 어떤 세계가 그에게 있다. 거기에 무슨 이름을 붙일 수 있을까? 그 '어떤'을 다 모은 세계는 어디로 향할 것인가? 잘 모르겠다.

　하지만 단 한 가지만은 명백해 보인다. 적어도 세계 혹은 일상의 양면성에 대한 인식의 냉철함, '생의 이면'

The classic stability of the narrative structure, delicate writing style that transfers subtle emotion, a strong perspective on existence and life. The literary landscape that these three strong threads have woven together has bursts of new energy that is not often found in Korean literary circles. Jung's literary world is more classical than Bae Su-ah's, calmer than Jeon Gyeong-rin's, more diversified than Gong Ji-young's, more stylish than Shin Kyung-sook's, and more desperate than Eun Hee-kyung's. What should we name it? If we put together all aspects of her literary world, where would it head to? I am not sure. But one thing is

을 보는 그의 집요한 시선이 분명한 출발이 될 것이라
는 사실 말이다.

박철화

정미경, 서하진, 정이현 등에 의해 주도되고 있는 최
근 우리 소설의 '부르주아 서사'는 부르주아의 취향과
내적 갈등, 그리고 삶의 방식 등에 있어서 이제까지 어
떤 소설들도 보여주지 못한 풍부한 디테일과 적절한 에
피소드 포착 능력 등을 자랑한다. 부르주아라는 하나의
유형으로 묶일 수 있는 그들 집단의 일련의 사적 영역
에 관한 유형화된 접근 방식, 예컨대 사랑과 결혼의 관
습, 가정을 관리하고 영위하는 기술, 가족 구성원 간의
관계 맺기의 양상, 그것이 한 시대와 맺고 있는 삶의 유
형 등이 이들에 의해 우리 소설사 속으로 진입하게 되었
다. 이로써 우리는 부르주아라는 추상적 집단 한가운데
를 흐르는 미시적인 삶의 실핏줄들을 확보하게 되었다.

신수정

새로운 감각으로 벼려진 정미경의 소설 언어는 진실
과 거짓, 성찰과 자기기만의 경계가 불분명해지는 영역

clear. Her cold awareness of the duality of the world or people's daily lives and her persistent perspective on the hidden sides of life will be a great starting point.

Park Cheol-hwa

The "bourgeoisie narrative" of Korean novels these days, advocated by Jung Mi-kyung, Seo Ha-jin, and Jeong Yi-hyun, boasts of abundant detail and the ability to capture appropriate episodes that no other novels and short stories have been able to illustrate. The "bourgeois" category, which refers to a series of their formalized approach toward privacy—for instance, the convention of love and marriage, the skills to manage and lead a family, the trend of relationship formation among family members, and the type of life these factors create in this age—has become a part of the Korean literary history through the aforementioned writers. As a result, we have been able to secure microscopic lines of thread that is interlaced in the center of this abstract group called the "bourgeois."

Shin Su-jeong

Jung Mi-kyung's language, forged with a new

에서 빛을 발한다. 따지고 보면 소설은 처음부터 근대적 개인의 자기기만과 타인에 대한 몰이해를 다뤄왔지만 만사가 돈의 위력에 휘둘려 세상도 사람의 속내도 뒤죽박죽인 요즘처럼 그 일이 절실할 때가 있으랴. (……) 우리 시대 사람들의 공감의 한계와 허위의식을 섬세하게 파고드는 정미경의 작품들이야말로 이런 소설 본연의 작업을 훌륭하게 해내고 있다는 사실이다.

한기욱

생의 이면이나 밑그림을 파헤쳐 그늘 속의 빛보다는 빛 속의 그늘을, 기쁨에서조차 우러나오는 삶의 슬픔을 감식해낼 수 있는 혜안이 이 작가에게는 있다. 견디기 힘든 것은 세상의 불완전함이 아니라 불완전함에 대한 혐오나 배척임을 아는 이 작가의 소설은, 그래서 의외로 차가우면서도 따뜻하다. 눈물처럼.

김미현

taste, shines when the boundary between truth and lie, and self-reflection and self-deception are blurred. Strictly speaking, fiction has dealt with the self-deception of the modern individual and their lack of understanding of others. However, it cannot be more desperately dealt with at any other time than today, when everything is swayed by the power of money, and the world and the people have all become jumbled up. [...] Jung's works, which delicately delve into the extend of people's sympathy toward others, as well as their false consciousness, are carrying out their true function as fiction.

Han Gi-uk

As she explores the hidden sides of life, Jung has the insight to identify shadows in the light instead of the light, and the sorrow that is welled up even in joy. Her story knows that it is not the deficiencies of this world but the hatred and antagonism of these deficiencies that are difficult for us to bear. That is the reason why her story is cold and objective and yet unexpectedly warm. Like tears.

Kim Mi-hyeon

정미경

정미경은 1960년 2월 4일 경상남도 마산에서 태어났다. 1978년 이화여자대학교 영어영문학과에 입학한 뒤에 정미경은 본격적으로 소설을 쓰기 시작한다. 이화여대 학보사에서 개최하는 이화문학상에 해마다 응모하여 단편, 중편, 희곡 부문에서 입상했으며, 고려대문학상을 수상하기도 한다.

그 후로 전개된 정미경의 문학적 이력은 독특하다. 두 번의 등단이 있었기 때문이다. 그녀는 1987년에 《중앙일보》 신춘문예 희곡 부문에 「폭설」이 당선되어 문단에 나왔지만, 소설가로서 본격적인 출발을 하게 된 것은 2001년 《세계의 문학》 소설 부문에 당선되면서부터였다. 1987년부터 2001년 사이, 오랜 공백이 있었던 셈이지만 늘 작가의 눈으로 보고 쓰는 훈련을 게을리하지 않았던 정미경은 이 공백 기간이 무색하리만치 왕성한 작품 활동을 벌인다. 그녀는 소설을 쓰며 보낸 이 시간들을 한 에세이에서 '전쟁 같은 세월'이었다고 회고한다. 친구도 만나지 않고 휴가를 가지도 않은 채 그녀는

Jung Mi-kyung

Jung Mi-kyung was born on February 4, 1960 in Masan, Gyeongsangnam-do. In 1978, she enrolled in Ewha University as a major in English and English Literature and began to write. She submitted her works to the Ewha Literary Competition, held by the *Ewha Weekly*, and received awards in the categories of short story, novella, and drama. She also received Korea University Literary Award.

Since then, Jung's literary career unfolded in an unusual manner. She made her official debut as a writer twice. She first debuted as a writer when her play "A Blizzard" was selected as a winner of *the Joongang Ilbo*'s Spring Literary Contest in 1987 in the drama category. However, her career as a true novelist began when her fiction was selected as the winner of *World Literature* in 2001. There was a huge gap for her between 1987 and 2001, but Jung always kept her perspective as a writer and made a constant effort to continue writing. She consistently wrote and published her work, enough to undermine the gap of 14 years in her career. In an essay,

줄기차게 작품을 발표했고, 그 결과 치밀한 관찰과 섬세한 문장, 그리고 부르주아 계급에 대한 새로운 시선을 지닌 작가로서 문단의 주목을 받게 된다.

그렇게 써낸 작품들의 대강을 살펴보면 다음과 같다. 소설집으로는 『나의 피투성이 연인』(2004), 『발칸의 장미를 내게 주었네』(2006), 『내 아들의 연인』(2008), 『프랑스식 세탁소』(2013)가 있으며, 장편소설로는 『장밋빛 인생』(2002), 『이상한 슬픔의 원더랜드』(2005), 『아프리카의 별』(2010)이 있다. 그중 『장밋빛 인생』으로 2002년에 제26회 오늘의 작가상을 수상했으며, 「밤이여, 나뉘어라」로 2006년에 제30회 이상문학상을 수상했다.

한 남자의 아내로서의 삶, 두 아들의 어머니로서의 삶, 그리고 소설가로서의 삶, 이 다양한 삶의 양상들이 정미경의 소설에 녹아들어 입체적인 시선과 구체적인 묘사를 가능하게 하는 것은 아닐까. 정미경은 한 매체와의 인터뷰에서 소설가는 "직업이라기보다는 그냥 어떤 '운명' 같다"고 말했다. 그 운명이 우리들에게 또 어떠한 소설을 가져다줄지, 계속 기대해본다.

she wrote that the time she spent writing short stories and novels was tantamount to "years of war." She continuously published her works, without meeting friends or going on a vacation. As a result, she began to receive the spotlight in the Korean literary world for her meticulous observation, delicate sentences, and a new perspective on the bourgeoisie.

Jung's major works are as follows: As for collections of short stories, there are *My Bloodied Lover* (2004), *He Gave Me Roses of the Balkans* (2006), *My Son's Lover* (2008), and *A French Laundromat* (2013). Her novels include *Life is Rosy* (2002), *A Strange Sorrowful Wonderland* (2005), and *An African Star* (2010).

Among them, Jung received the Writer of Today Award in 2002 with "Life is Rosy," and the Yi Sang Literary Award in 2006 with her short story "Night, Be Divided."

Various aspects of her life—a wife, a mother of two sons, and a novelist—have melted into her writing, and they are probably what enables her to keep a dynamic perspective and detailed descriptions in her works. In an interview, Jung said that being a writer is "like a 'destiny' than having a job." We hope to continue being excited about the kind of novels and short stories her "destiny" will bring us.

번역 **스텔라 김** Translated by Stella Kim

스텔라 김은 콜비대학교에서 음악과 동아시아학을, 컬럼비아대학교에서 한국 역사를 공부했다. 한국문학번역원의 정규과정을 통해 문학 번역을 접하고 깊은 관심을 갖게 되었다. 현재 한국외국어대학교 통번역대학원에 재학 중이며 프리랜서 통번역가로 활동하고 있다.

Stella Kim studied Music and East Asian Studies at Colby College and Korean History at Columbia University in the City of New York. She developed her interest in literary translation while spending a year in the Translation Academy at the Literature Translation Institute of Korea. Currently, she is studying at the Graduate School of Interpretation and Translation at Hankuk University of Foreign Studies and is also working as a freelance interpreter/translator.

감수 **전승희, 데이비드 윌리엄 홍**

Edited by Jeon Seung-hee and David William Hong

전승희는 서울대학교와 하버드대학교에서 영문학과 비교문학으로 박사 학위를 받았으며, 현재 하버드대학교 한국학 연구소의 연구원으로 재직하며 아시아 문예 계간지 《ASIA》 편집위원으로 활동 중이다. 현대 한국문학 및 세계문학을 다룬 논문을 다수 발표했으며, 바흐친의 『장편소설과 민중언어』, 제인 오스틴의 『오만과 편견』 등을 공역했다. 1988년 한국여성연구소의 창립과 《여성과 사회》의 창간에 참여했고, 2002년부터 보스턴 지역 피학대 여성을 위한 단체인 '트랜지션하우스' 운영에 참여해 왔다. 2006년 하버드대학교 한국학 연구소에서 '한국 현대사와 기억'을 주제로 한 워크숍을 주관했다.

Jeon Seung-hee is a member of the Editorial Board of *ASIA*, and a Fellow at the Korea Institute, Harvard University. She received a Ph.D. in English Literature from Seoul National University and a Ph.D. in Comparative Literature from Harvard University. She has presented and published numerous papers on modern Korean and world literature. She is also a co-translator of Mikhail Bakhtin's *Novel and the People's Culture* and Jane Austen's *Pride and Prejudice*. She is a founding member of the Korean Women's Studies Institute and of the biannual Women's Studies' journal *Women and Society* (1988), and she has been working at 'Transition House,' the first and oldest shelter for battered women in New England. She organized a workshop entitled "The Politics of Memory in Modern Korea" at the Korea Institute, Harvard University, in 2006. She also served as an advising committee member for the Asia-Africa Literature Festival in 2007 and for the POSCO Asian Literature Forum in 2008.

데이비드 윌리엄 홍은 미국 일리노이주 시카고에서 태어났다. 일리노이대학교에서 영문학을, 뉴욕대학교에서 영어교육을 공부했다. 지난 2년간 서울에 거주하면서 처음으로 한국인과 아시아계 미국인 문학에 깊이 몰두할 기회를 가졌다. 현재 뉴욕에서 거주하며 강의와 저술 활동을 한다.

David William Hong was born in 1986 in Chicago, Illinois. He studied English Literature at the University of Illinois and English Education at New York University. For the past two years, he lived in Seoul, South Korea, where he was able to immerse himself in Korean and Asian-American literature for the first time. Currently, he lives in New York City, teaching and writing.

바이링궐 에디션 한국 대표 소설 072
발칸의 장미를 내게 주었네

2014년 6월 6일 초판 1쇄 인쇄 | 2014년 6월 13일 초판 1쇄 발행

지은이 정미경 | **옮긴이** 스텔라 김 | **펴낸이** 김재범
감수 전승희, 데이비드 윌리엄 홍 | **기획** 정은경, 전성태, 이경재
편집 정수인, 이은혜 | **관리** 박신영 | **디자인** 이춘희
펴낸곳 (주)아시아 | **출판등록** 2006년 1월 27일 제406-2006-000004호
주소 서울특별시 동작구 서달로 161-1(흑석동 100-16)
전화 02.821.5055 | **팩스** 02.821.5057 | **홈페이지** www.bookasia.org
ISBN 979-11-5662-018-1 (set) | 979-11-5662-034-1 (04810)
값은 뒤표지에 있습니다.

Bi-lingual Edition Modern Korean Literature 072
He Gave Me Roses of the Balkans

Written by Jung Mi-kyung | **Translated by** Stella Kim
Published by Asia Publishers | 161-1, Seodal-ro, Dongjak-gu, Seoul, Korea
Homepage Address www.bookasia.org | **Tel.** (822).821.5055 | **Fax.** (822).821.5057
First published in Korea by Asia Publishers 2014
ISBN 979-11-5662-018-1 (set) | 979-11-5662-034-1 (04810)

바이링궐 에디션 한국 대표 소설 set 4

디아스포라 Diaspora

가족 Family

유머 Humor